aliterate

Volume 1, Fall 2016

aliterate

Volume 1, Fall 2016

Edited by
Brendan Hickey // Emilio T. Jasso // Joshua L. Pevner

Staff

Brendan Hickey
Emilio T. Jasso
Joshua L. Pevner
Dustin W. Funk
Alicia Kort
R.S. Mason
Michael D. Williams

Acknowledgements

Ken Alba
Franco Alvarado
Alice H.R.H. Beckwith
Brian Hickey
Alina Kononov
Mary Soon Lee
Jonathan Ostrowsky
Ralan
Joe Stech
David Steffen
Jeremy Trout

ISBN-10: 1-945923-00-8
ISBN-13: 978-1-945923-00-5
ISSN 2471-4593
©2016 All Rights Reserved
Introduction ©2016 Shariann Lewitt
A Companion for the Stars ©2016 Diana Estigarribia
Beyond the Sea ©2016 Nick Tchan
Desert Stand ©2016 Richard C. Rogers
Joined ©2016 Sarah L. Byrne
Memento Vivere ©2016 Elian Crane
Rubble People ©2016 Matthew Sanborn Smith
The Asteroid Man ©2016 Kuldar Leement

aliterate is a production of Genre, Ltd., a 501(c)3 non-profit organization chartered in the Commonwealth of Massachusetts.

Selected Correspondence: *Books for sale. For lists contact E. Francis. 47 Nassen Road, Saltley B8 3JP England.*

aliterate (*n*) – one who can, but does not, read

Contents

FOREWORD

Shariann Lewitt

There have always been stories. As far back as we can trace in this history of our species, in every culture on our planet, people have told, written, recited, and acted them out. Our stories teach us who we are, who we want to be, and who we can become.

You hold in your hands a collection of fine stories, stories that stand at the crossroad of the best in genre and literary storytelling.

You are also looking at a historic crossroad of two converging sensibilities in our perceptions of literature as well. Once upon a time there were two kinds of stories, the kind people liked and the kind they didn't. The kind they liked got told over and over again. The kind they didn't died—or got relegated to the heap of minutia that in the best case become dissertations for desperate doctoral candidates. But then the binary changed. Somehow we ended up with Literature and, well, commercial writing (i.e., genre.)

That progression has some clear markers along the way. In the 1920s, important literary writer of the day Sherwood Anderson railed against the tyranny of plot and argued for deeper, more meaningful presentation of character in the short stories of the day. Today the modern literary story focuses on character and minute observation of emotional nuance told in beautiful language. One acquaintance said that, in her MFA Fiction program, a professor started out by saying something to the effect that everyone agreed that the short story illustrated a slice of life and there was no longer any need for discussion on this point.

Meanwhile, all that plot stuff went into genre. At the same time that Sherwood Anderson excoriated the tyranny of plot, legendary science fiction editor Hugo Gernsback started Amazing Stories, the first science fiction genre magazine. His stated purpose was to attract boys to careers in engineering. A running joke in the genre is that the Golden Age of SF is thirteen. Many of the early stories in Amazing and the many other magazines that followed were, indeed, dreadful. Wooden characters, grade school grammar and long explanations of science and engineering all in service to almighty plot—no wonder the literati at the New Yorker looked down on genre and genre writers from the heights of the Algonquin Room.

But Hugo Gernsback was not the only editor, science fiction was not the only genre, and the 1920s and 30s were not the only decades. While no one in the literary world watched, genre grew up. Science fiction and fantasy, noir and mystery (which always did have somewhat more cachet), even westerns started to dig deeper into nuances of character and emotion while the writers in these genres started to gain more mastery of language.

In the sixties the tide began to turn. In Science Fiction, the New Wave brought strong literary values to the forefront of the genre. While there had always been a few writers of high caliber, the nineteen sixties saw a shift in vision of what this genre could and should be. Writers married the longtime concern with plot and storytelling (and science and engineering) with character and worldbuilding and attention to language. More writers came from literary backgrounds, and those who didn't read serious fiction and mastered finer style.

And then came DHALGREN. Yes, there were other books and other authors, but Samuel R. Delaney's work put character front and center. And his prose often bordered on poetry. Sometimes you just had to read his sentences aloud for the pleasure of the language. No one could argue but that Delaney was and is a literary writer, an iconoclast, and a visionary. He was by no means the only truly literary writer to shake up the literary world's perception of genre, and the genre's perception of itself, but he was and remains among the most vital, the most outspoken, the most long lasting.

You hold in your hands his great-grandchild, mixed with DNA stolen from the NEW YORKER and from ELLERY QUEEN too. Because the editors of Aliterate have created a magazine where they have gone back to the first binary. They have chosen tales with nuanced characters and beautiful language. And rip-roaring good stories, too, because they like stories.

Once upon a time there were stories that people liked and those that people didn't like. I think you will like these stories. Very much.

INTRODUCTION
The Editors

Welcome to Aliterate. Inside you'll find stories by the *realists of a larger reality*[1].

Some may ask: Why another magazine dedicated to genre fiction, and what is literary genre fiction?

To the first question: we enjoy it and want to read more of it. We hope in earnest that you agree.

Our answer to the second question is a bit longer.

Contemporary American literature is dominated by the literary realists, who trace their heritage back to writers such as Pushkin, Balzac, and Flaubert. Realism came of age through the pens of Hemingway, Faulker, Bellow, O'Connor, and other giants of the 20th century canon. Style and beauty triumphed while a good plot became hard to find.

While literary realism flourished, the so-called genres–science fiction, fantasy, horror, the Western, pulps, romance, crime–enjoyed their own golden age with Clarke, Asimov, Heinlein, and many more familiar names. However, while the space opera's swashbuck-

---

[1]Ursula K. Le Guin, National Book Award Speech, 2014.

ler triumphed, the pulp novel did few favors for the field's reputation as 'serious writing'. While some criticisms of genre fiction are driven purely by snobbishness, it would be lazy to ignore all of them.

As the golden age of genre waned, it gave way to something remarkable: Atwood, Delany, and Le Guin emerged with prose as illuminating as their ideas. Borges and his rival Sabato appeared in English. Genre fiction crept into the mainstream, disguised in the magical realism of writers like Milhauser. This is the writing that excites us. It appropriates the technical lessons of the realists and executes within the outline of genre writing[2]. Today we see brighter flickers of this transcendent writing. With this publication we hope to highlight brilliant writing at this intersection and offer something to both the fan of contemporary realism and those who swear by fantasy and science fiction.

With that, we'll stand aside and let the writers herein speak.

–The Editors

---

[2]Verlyn Klinkenborg writes in *Several Short Sentences on Writing*: "But genres are merely outlines by another name."

A Companion for the Stars

Diana Estigarribia

The harness restricts my movements, and I am only able to turn my head back and forth. I strain against the chains, pushing my face towards the ventilator. The capsule grows hotter with every passing minute, the air running out. I must find a way to tell them something's gone wrong.

Tell them to bring me home before it's too late.

Instead, the voice talks about me as if I can't hear him. Yes, I'm still here, I'm still alive. The voice drones on: "Tral-D telemetry ongoing, spectro-photometers measuring cosmic and ultraviolet rays. Data confirmed, next check fifteen minutes after each orbit."

Strange words I once overheard in the laboratory. I close my eyes and focus on my exercises. Despite the months of preparation and training, it is frightening to feel so helpless. Even the utmost concentration cannot drown out the continuous rattling and pounding on the tiny panels that surround me.

There's no food left now, having eaten the salty, gelatinized substance after takeoff. No water either—I've pulled at the tube dangling above my left eye and extracted every bit of moisture.

And I'm still not sure how I've come to find myself here.

Before, I was self-sufficient, living on the streets and surviving by my wits. I slept in alleys and rode the Metro at night to stay warm. Around me, the roar of Moscow: automobiles, buses, *elektrichika* streetcars, horses and trolleys—though they say there is only one left now—a relentless churning, a city in constant agitation, on the edge of snapping and breaking. I stayed out of its way in the crevices, in the shadows.

That changed when I was taken in by the old baker on Arbat street, who ran an inconspicuous establishment with a single oven and wood-planked floors snowy white with powder. It was warm in the winter, away from the cold wind and rain. The baker fed me *vatrushka* buns and baked apples. He let me sleep inside by the sugar sacks, as long as I didn't lick them. From daybreak to long into the evening, the bakery filled with the sweet-and-sour aromas of molasses and coriander. People came from all over the city for his loaves of black bread and *moskovsky kalatch*.

When did you get a pet, Evgeny, the regular customers asked. *She is so charming*, they said, and called me *tiny one, shy one*. Sometimes I got an affectionate pat on the head or a small treat. Nearly a year went by, and it was the happiest time of my life.

I thought the baker might ask me to live with him, but every night he showed me the door—shoved me outside and did not offer to take me home. This meant sleeping on the trains again, or waiting by the door until morning. Then I discovered I was pregnant. The baker screamed and kicked me. When his assistants tried to help, he shouted at them too. I ran away as fast as I could and wandered, lost and ashamed.

Is it so hard to believe I trusted the other man when he held out his hand? "Don't be afraid, *limonchik*," he said, *little curly one*. I had nothing and nowhere to go. I didn't want to give birth alone. Finally, I thought, I've found a safe haven for myself and my new family. But I never saw my pups again.

I didn't understand until later that the man had come searching for a case like mine, to take advantage of my rootlessness. To be without a home is more than lacking shelter; it means your life is precarious, usually in peril, and you make ill-informed choices.

The man took me to an isolated place outside the city, a cold, unfriendly building filled with instruments and machines and sour faced, pale people in white coats. As soon as I arrived I lost all my freedom, was watched and penned in, a prisoner who didn't know her crime.

It was here I first heard their odd talk, and learned I was to be a "test subject." I was afraid of what this might mean, and of them.

Their huge, icy hands prodded and poked my body. They tested my urine and feces, shone lights in my eyes and put mechanical devices in my ears and throat. My diet was limited and I knew hunger again, and only when the scale read six kilograms did it please them. I wondered if they were deliberately shrinking me, making me smaller as part of their cruel experiments.

In the beginning, I was let out once in the late mornings, always under their watchful eye. Eventually, even that glimpse of freedom was taken from me. Day by day, they moved me to smaller and smaller cages. I tracked time in captivity by scratching a line in the bottom of the cages for each day. In the first I made ten lines. The next, fifteen lines. And in the final cage I marked out twenty days.

On the two-hundred fortieth day, I met others like me. There were three of us altogether, all females. Perhaps we knew one another from the streets, perhaps not—it was better to pretend to be strangers.

The one called Albina eyed me warily, growling with a low sound in her throat; I responded with my loudest bark.

Some of the men began to laugh, the women in the room joining in. One looked at me and said, "you have quite a voice for such a little thing!" And that's when they gave me my name—I was to be known thereafter as "the barker." I had never had a name before, not even on Arbat Street.

I did not like having this sudden reputation for being loud. But as much as I tried to be friendly, my overtures were met with indifference.

I envied the one they named Myshka because a paw correctly pressed against a panel or nose tapped instrument rewarded her with an extra treat or affection. But I suspected this was a way to manipulate her. I advised Myshka not to trust as easily as I had. The more I wanted to convince her we couldn't trust these men, the more she whimpered. As if to confirm my warning, they soon confined her to a dark, airless box and abandoned her there for hours.

Myshka cried great wails and sobs all night, begging to be brought back into their good graces. And when they eventually left us all in the dark, I remained quiet and tried to sleep, even though hearing Myshka so distressed upset me as well. She rejected my offerings of comfort; she didn't seem to understand me.

We could discern no clues from the curious activities we endured. One day they walked me to the end of a long hallway and into a large space with a metal plank extending the breadth of the room. Attached to the end of the plank was a round bag connected to two gear boxes. They strapped a soft harness around my torso and body, leaving my limbs exposed, and then slid me inside the odd apparatus.

A young woman appeared carrying a glass globe which she fit over my head, locking it in place. She smiled at me and told me to stay. Everyone moved to the perimeter of the room. After a few moments, the metal plank and I began to rotate, faster and faster, until my masters' faces blurred and I felt an immense weight pressing against me. This ordeal continued daily for the next five days.

Not once were we told why they were doing this, what our purpose was.

Then, as if by miracle, yesterday it all stopped—and the same man who found me took me to his home. There I played with his two children. They wrapped their pudgy arms around my neck and treated me like family. I ate *vatrushka buns* and felt like myself again. I rejoiced, feeling lighter than ever and I wanted to jump up forever. It was everything I had ever dreamed of having. To thank him I tried to kiss and lick the man's face, but he was serious, focusing on something past me.

I understand now he was saying goodbye.

We returned to the laboratory and I admit I felt a great emptiness. There was no time to mourn my glimpse of happiness and freedom, however, as more preparation followed at a breakneck speed. This is when I learned the great undertaking was not to happen here. I was bundled up and we traveled many, many kilometers to another place. I glimpsed it briefly: a vast open steppe, barren and gray. There was no city here, no people conducting their business, only metal girders and empty rail tracks.

Outside the fading night sky stayed blue, the stars blinking, winking at me. Were they tired like me? Sleepy, I yawned, my tongue wagging. Am I to get breakfast?

Nervous energy permeated my masters' actions. I nuzzled the hands of those who carried me, attempted to kiss their worried faces, but they were stone-faced.

For the first time I saw the craft, a kind of miniature house coming to a point, resembling the ones on Pushkin Square. Unlike an automobile there are no wheels and no seating. There is one door that opens outward, a kind of hatch. Even if I wanted to push it open, it looks much too heavy to move.

They produced another harness and strapped it around my body. They inserted a bag directly underneath me. Am I not even to get walked this morning? One of the white coats told me to stay calm as he attached small, padded patches to my chest and legs, which were then connected to other wires.

And to my utter shock, they secured me in heavy chains.

I started barking, louder and louder. I even considered biting them. I couldn't have, of course, but I felt no reason to be treated this way. What had I done? But it was no use. I was completely at the mercy of my caretakers, as I had been since that fateful day in Moscow.

One last task remained before they sealed me inside. A photographer and film crew recorded the occasion. In the city a passerby might take a photograph of me now and again, and every time I hoped to get something in return: a treat, or water, or a modicum of affection, but they only pointed and mocked me.

Today I put on my bravest, most attractive expression, my head straight, my ears pointed and my eyes bright. I stood tall, my face tilted upwards in a most heroic pose. Everyone took turns getting a photo with me and the capsule.

But none of them were interested in praising me or acknowledging my hard work and sacrifice—only the capsule and its mysterious instruments held their attention. The men once again regarded me with stern expressions and anxious faces, their brows furrowed. At least no one laughed.

They closed the hatch and with a whoosh of air, I was sealed in airtight. I could hear myself breathing in the capsule.

The act of enclosing me inside the craft was the moment of epiphany. Now I knew what my task would be. It was clear I would be going on a journey of great importance. Out of everyone, I was chosen. I had triumphed over Albina and Myshka.

Now everyone will be watching. Everyone will know me.

Back home, on this bright, clear, beautiful day of blue cloudless skies, the pack must be riding the Metro to ward off the chill and pleading for meals in the streets.

But there was not a moment to spare. I was moved to a very large structure and lifted onto a metal gurney, and we traveled through brightly lit corridors, emerging outside. I moved back and forth but couldn't see much outside of the little window above my head. Moving quickly, feet shuffling, the others spin and coast like leaves caught in a squall. Like a leaf torn off its branch, I was buoyed along in the direction of my destiny.

After attaching cables and hoses, the men placed my craft onto a pad and stepped away. The doors were shut and locked with great effort, and at last, I was alone.

Then, the most shattering noise, a huge rumbling sound, louder than anything I'd ever heard. I worried the shaking would break me, destroy me, that my heart would beat so fast it would burst through my chest. The very doorway vibrated. The air was superheated. The cabin shook and moved violently, and I was sure it would explode.

Do not leave me here, come get me, come get me! I thought, and then, *no, I will not be like Myshka; I will be strong.*

My heart raced—hundreds of times a minute, as if I was running for my life, but there's no one pursuing me. My heart beats so fast it's erupting from my chest. Can't calm my breathing.

Breathing so shallow and fast, hyperventilating, surely I will die–when the voice, his voice, comes through the panel in front of me.

"All right, *limonchik*. It will be over soon, *Zhuchka*, my little bug."

And then I lift ever higher, propelled into the sky, higher and higher, through misty clouds and then suddenly darkness, darkness in the middle of the day.

Darkness, but not night. The sky is an infinite blackness deeper and darker than any night I've ever seen. It is so very, very black— blacker than newly shined soldier's boots, deeper than fresh tar on the roads. Darkness that is blinding, that hurts to look at, an omnipresence gazing back at you, indifferent, merciless. It was daylight when I left them. The blinking and winking stars are so much closer. There are so many stars.

And again it's dawn, the window filling with rose-pinks and fiery oranges. Glowing sunset followed by glowing sunrise. It gives way to night once more. Time has no meaning.

I am far away, and yet my home feels so near.

And now I have an understanding: I am not bound to the ground. This is where I have been all along, running over the surface of an immense creation, a domain so vast as to not be believed—but my own eyes perceive it.

Color fills the craft, greens and grays and whites—walls of water and clouds. The great curve of the world is revealed to me, and above it, a thin seam embracing the planet in a halo of light, protecting us from the unrelenting blackness.

I am moving incredibly fast. I am untethered, speeding across the sky. The journey reminds me of the great hunts of legend. Prey, pursuit, heartbeat roaring in my ears. Where is my master to accompany me on my journey? How will I find her?

A brilliant white star with a blue-ish tinge there—perhaps I'm not alone.

Speaking out my observations as clearly as I can, I tap with my paws and press my nose to the panel. Above the instruments is a glass, hundreds of lines filling a tiny frame.

The heat is unbearable now. The fan no longer functions. The cabin is stultifying, suffocating me. Walls becoming thinner somehow. When everything shook and a piece of my metal sphere separated, parts of the insulated walls tore. This little house of mine is being torn apart.

Looking away, moving faster second by second, I come to realize these passes over the world move me closer to my end.

Still my new, brightest friend sparkles. My touchstone. Spinning golden clusters.

I am a wave of light, like an arrow, rising into the sky. I am an explorer, no longer of the nooks and alleyways of my city. There is so much more. I had no idea how vast the world is.

In my former home, would the old streets seem small to me? The streets I know so well: there I'll hide in the old alleys during the morning drizzle and watch the people jostle with their umbrellas; there I'll see the young boys and girls flirting in their open-topped cars; an errand boy with a loaf of bread tucked under each arm; the soldiers stopping for ice cream during the May Day parade. May or November, summer or winter, the people live and work and love and die. And I'll see them.

Here there are no seasons, no cold or heat or wind or rain. Only a terrible tranquility and silence. I was a wanderer, ever-moving from place to place, with no particular home. There was freedom, yes; but also loneliness. No loneliness is as great as that when surrounded by others who do not see you.

I have come to that loneliest place of all, that which is hidden inside. The place we look away from and are frightened to face. No one should be alone there. Instead of closing our hearts to ourselves, we must expand, widening the senses. This must be the purpose of my journey: the expansion of ourselves beyond our existence as it is now. To journey forever and be a companion for others so they don't feel the loneliness in the darkness.

Am I meant to transform? No, I already am that which I am, I only need to become as I already was. A full circle of becoming, a whole existence. My existence is an untapped potentiality. I have earned my worth.

I am no longer an individual, no longer separate, but I am stretched to a wavelength made of my own sinew and muscle, a membrane of an immeasurable body in the firmament.

Whenever anyone looks up at the night sky, they will see me, shining bright in the darkness. I will be as the myriad dots of light.

Close your eyes, see me everywhere.

All of you strong, curious, searching hunters, you will look up and see me. You will say, there is our little *Zhuchka*, no longer our little bug. There is our steadfast companion. There she is.

Joined

Sarah L. Byrne

When your heart broke, I felt it too. We were walking through the city park when it happened; together but apart, because that was the way we'd become by then, wasn't it? There was an arm's-length distance and a silence as wide as a desert between us, but we were still joined, which meant we were sharing the scent of the lilac blossoms, the cool of the spring air on our skin, sharing the guarded edges of each other's feelings. Then your heart just tore itself apart.

It wasn't exactly your heart, I know–that's poetic license I'd add in later, because you weren't around to do it–but it was close enough. A catastrophic aortic rupture. But because we were joined, I felt the tearing pain rip through your body, and for a moment my breath choked off as the blood drained from your aorta into your chest. But only for a moment. My blood pressure fell only enough that I sank slowly to my knees on the gravel, while yours dropped to nothing as you crumpled to the ground. My heart went on beating while yours gave a last desperate flutter then just stopped.

Voices, footsteps, people rushing to surround you as you lay there on your back in the middle of the path, your skin waxy pale, your eyes open and dilated black. You were already gone. They didn't know it, but I did. I felt it happen.

Now I feel nothing.

It was a strange experience for a while, this feeling nothing. At least, if nothing is what you can call it. Feeling only my own feelings, thinking my own thoughts; alone in my own head after so long. The nothing I'd wanted for so long.

Six years back when we got our license, getting joined had seemed like such a romantic idea: for your partner to be truly your other half, to share each other's everyday joys and sorrows, to literally feel each other's pain and pleasure, one brain to the other through a real-time upload and download. So we registered, one of the first couples to do it, along with the marriage license– I, Tracy, do take you, Alana–and received our neural implants, just a painless injection, harmless nanoparticles that targeted the nerve fibres and grew rapidly along them, twined around them like wisteria, no different from the kind they use for paralysis and prosthetics. Then in only a matter of weeks we were fully joined.

Sex was double the fun, of course. That's what everyone wanted to talk about at first, but for some of us it went further. Beyond sharing physical sensations and basic emotions, into thoughts and memories too. Even dreams, because wasn't it all the same thing really? All just neural connections, electrical impulses jumping synaptic gaps and neuropeptides docking with receptors. All of it picked up, encoded and transmitted by the implant.

It would be impossible to hurt each other, when you were joined, that's what people said. They were wrong: it wasn't just possible, it was easy. No, it was more than easy; it was inevitable. In those days we were wound so tight around each other it was hard to believe we were separate people. So you knew when things started changing between us, because I had no secrets from you–but you didn't want to know. You didn't want to know how cloying I'd begun to find your presence, pretending not to notice how my mind flinched away from yours when you reached out to me. And I pretending not to feel your hurt. It was grotesque, wasn't it? But we went on for more than a year like that, alone together, until that day your heart finally broke.

I lied when I said I felt nothing that day. What I felt was relief.

I'm trying to sleep in the attic room under the roof windows, like I usually do these nights. I like it up here under the sky, and since you've been gone, the thought of sleeping alone in the bed we used to share is unthinkable. Tonight, it's one of those clear summer nights when the temperature drops, the stars come out clear and the heat of the day fades into refreshing coolness. I'll get to sleep eventually, even with it playing over and over in my mind like it does most nights: you falling away from me, falling out of me; the life fading out of your eyes, the blood draining out of your heart.

We were told that a weakening of the arteries was a rare risk of the implants. Your blood pressure must have been too high. You knew you were supposed to quit smoking after we were joined, but you never could. You tried–for me, mostly, because I didn't like the taste–but somehow you never quite could give it up. I still felt the desperation of your cravings too as they clawed at you over the hours and the days: so I gave in. We called it a compromise.

Now, I block out the thought of the pack of cigarettes in the drawer downstairs. Sleep comes.

It's a feeling that wakes me. Cold. I turn over in bed, tugging the sheet up around my bare shoulder. Did I leave a window open? No. I did not. But there's a coldness creeping over my skin still. It's distant and alien, still entirely familiar.

"Alana?"

"I'm cold," you say. Or don't say, but you think it and my brain responds to your thought. Your feelings flood my senses, the old intensity of them, and for a moment it's like it always was.

But it's not.

"You're not real," I say into the empty darkness.

There's a hesitation, then your thought comes at me heavy with accusation, hits me hard. There'd be that little catch in your voice now if you still had one; there'd be hurt in your blue eyes if they weren't burned to ashes and scattered on the cold earth. And I'd look away.

"How can you say that?" you demand. "Don't you understand what's happening? I've come back to you. Tracy, don't you want us to be together again?"

I do, of course I do, that part of me that's lost its other half. The part of me that wants to believe death isn't a black oblivion waiting for all of us someday, maybe sooner than we think. The part that grieves for all those years back then when we were happy, for laughter and dancing, sex and snuggling under a blanket together, or staying up half the night sharing thoughts and feelings because it was like a well of cool water, yet however deep we drank we couldn't get enough of each other. There's an ache inside me, how badly I want that again.

But it wasn't like that towards the end. It was over. I know it and you know it too. Or you would if you were really here, if there was any you anymore.

You've gone quiet now. I don't feel anything from you. I curl up on my side and try to sleep again. But no matter what I do now, I just can't get warm.

Everything seems better in the morning, doesn't it always? I call the customer helpline to report the bug. My dead wife is in my head, I explain. She's talking to me. Something's gone wrong, some data cached in the system that should have been deleted; outdated settings somewhere in the cloud.

"Mmm-hmm," the bored sounding assistant on the other end of the line says, like it's some everyday thing. "We'll look into it for you."

Maybe this happens a lot. Maybe he doesn't believe a word of it. Most likely he's just sticking to his script and doesn't care particularly either way. Why should he, after all?

You come again that night.

"I'm cold," you say. "I want to come back. I want us to be together again."

"That's not possible."

"Maybe it is. We've got to try, haven't we? We've been given a second chance, surely it's happening for a reason?"

"I was going to leave you," I say. "It wasn't working out. We were going to separate, you knew that. We both knew."

"No," you say. A flood of images and feelings surge through me before I can stop you–happy times, good times, rose-tinted smiles– and I shove them back at you.

"Yes." You never could face a truth you didn't like, could you? "Alana, listen, I didn't want it to happen like this. I wanted you to be happy. I hoped you'd meet someone else, forget about me–"

"That would never have happened." You cut me off with a pulse of thought so sharp it hurts. "I'm not like you. I can't just switch off my feelings."

And apparently I can't switch off your feelings either.

I turn over, bury my face in the pillow. If you were here, for real, I'd feel your touch now. Your fingers sliding down my shoulders, the warmth of your body against mine, the scent of your hair. I'd feel what you feel and know you felt it right back; I'd hate myself for it but I'd turn over and pull you down to me. But you're not here. I don't know why I'm even having this conversation.

It's a while before you speak again: "Just do one thing for me."

"What?"

"I need a smoke. Just one. I'm desperate."

I let my breath out slowly against the pillow. We both know you've got me.

"All right."

I get out of bed, make my way downstairs and outside. I light the cigarette in the garden, awkward and clumsy despite the familiar feel of it against my fingers and lips, but when I inhale the sudden burn of the hot smoke in my lungs makes me cough it out sharply.

"Slowly," you tell me, your mind taut with impatience, with need. I breathe the smoke in steadily, holding it inside me this time, and feel the familiar nicotine-adrenaline rush through my veins, the familiar relief that's yours, not mine.

"Don't you miss this too?" you ask.

"No," I lie, letting the smoke out slowly. I take another drag.

If you could still smile, you would. You can't, but when you do, I feel it all the same.

It was a mistake, letting you have that one smoke. But then it was always a mistake to let you have your way, giving in to one of your 'compromises'. You had a way of sensing weakness, and you'd push for more, always more, never satisfied with what I could give you.

You come to me in the daytime now, as well as at night. You're there when I wake up, craving your morning coffee; you know I hate coffee, but somehow the smell of it drifts through my kitchen every morning these days. When I'm dressing, you're there with suggestions of perfume, how you miss it. Silk camisoles like you used to wear under your shirts, the smoothness against your skin. Darling, why don't you try your hair like this?

And now here I am, huddled under a flimsy shelter outside the entrance to the hospital where I'm supposed to be at work. My coat collar turned up against the wind, hands cupped around the dwindling end of a cigarette to protect it from the driving rain.

"Hey, Tracy. I didn't know you smoked."

I look up, startled, one of my co-workers standing there. I don't recognise him for a moment.

"I don't," I manage to say eventually.

He quirks an eyebrow before walking on, and I drop what's left of the cigarette, without looking down to see it fizzle out on the wet tarmac. I turn and head into the building.

I know what you want, Alana. To use my body, for us to share it. We're half-way there already.

But I'm saying no to you this time. Brushing the drops of water out of my hair and pulling off my wet jacket, I walk to my lab with more purpose than I have had in the months since this all started, because now I know what I have to do.

I shrug into my lab coat, glance at the samples waiting on my bench. I've always done my job in a detached way. It's just samples to analyse; blood in a vial, cells on a plate. I've made a point of not really thinking about where they come from. But that doesn't change the facts. There are dead people in the basement.

You want a body, Alana? I'll find you one. One all of your own. I'll inject you into it, you can worm your way through its veins, animate its dead nerves.

Just stay out of mine.

It's cold down here. I feel the chill as soon as I step out of the elevator, into this underground place where the dead people are.

"Help you?" The uninterested desk clerk glances up. I don't know her, she doesn't know me, but a glimpse of my lab coat and badge is enough that she's not going to ask difficult questions.

"Some samples didn't make it upstairs this morning, I need to talk to Mark," I lie.

It isn't difficult. If I can lie to my telepathic dead wife in my head–if I can lie so well to myself–it was never going to be hard to lie a stranger.

"He's inside." she says.

"Thanks."

I slide past the closed door of Mark's examination room, where he's conducting an autopsy, murmuring reports into his recording device. Down to the end of the corridor and into the storage room at the back. I pull on nitrile gloves, tug open one of the drawers, stare at the dead man, the stranger lying there. The cold body that doesn't look like anything that was ever alive, or ever will be again.

This is not going to be any use, I realise. I don't know what I was thinking, how I thought this was going to work, what I'm doing here. It never even made any sense. I push the drawer closed, start to turn away. But then I'm pulling open another drawer, and then another.

It's not me doing it. You're in my head. Suddenly, down here in the chill of this windowless cavern, you're here, guiding me, moving my hands for me. Drawing me to you.

Because when I open the third drawer, I stop, heart thudding against my ribs so hard it stops my breath.

Alana.

It's you. Just like you looked lying on the gravel under the lilacs that day.

You can't be here. I said my goodbyes to you. I organised the memorial service, stood there tearless with your parents weeping and casting me haunted looks–the one who broke their daughter's heart, who sent tendrils creeping through her veins to tie her forever to me and beguiled her to her death–if only they knew how it really was. I received your ashes in a wooden urn, startlingly heavy, to scatter in the park where we walked that day under the lilacs. Joined corpses have to be cremated for fear of contamination, irrational dread of the nanothings creeping free and making their way through the earth to wreak some unknown havoc. It couldn't happen, of course, they die when we do. Except when they don't.

You touch me, your fingertip down the back of my neck.

I tear off my gloves, turn and run into the corridor, and straight into Mark. He grabs me to steady me.

"Hey, Tracy, you all right?"

I jerk away from his touch, because it feels so wrong, so alien, to have anyone touch me but you. I find my breath, my voice, and it comes out harsh and angry.

"What's Alana doing here? She's not supposed to be here."

"What?"

He's staring at me like I've gone crazy, and I can't blame him, the way I must look.

I shoulder past him and don't look back, just keep walking until I'm outside. I breathe in the air, the summer storm clearing now to leave a clean-washed blue sky and the sun breaking through the last rain drops.

I wonder if I might really be going crazy. Because the implant can do that to a person; as well as breaking your heart, it can send your mind spooling loose into free fall. There've been documented cases, and I feel myself falling now, endlessly falling, and I'd grab at anything in desperation. I wonder if that's how you feel, drifting formless in the void.

I can't blame you for grabbing onto me like you did. Can't blame you at all.

I want you, suddenly, Alana. Want to hold you close and not let go, because I'm falling. Nothing makes sense anymore and I'm just falling.

It was a mistake, it turns out. An administrative error, they say. Your body was mixed up with another woman's: someone else's daughter, someone else's wife. A body that was supposed to be donated to science, but instead ended up burnt to ashes, scattered under the lilacs and denied my tears. These things happen, they say.

And that left you still there, cold and waiting in that drawer. Your implant still functioning–perhaps–still reaching out from that dark place, still calling out to me. Although that shouldn't really be possible. Maybe it isn't. Maybe it was only ever my circuitry reaching out, trailing through the empty space inside me, twisting back on itself?

Either way, it all gets sorted out in time, as such things always do. Compensation paid and apologies made, paperwork redone. The body–your body–cremated for real this time.

Life goes on.

I don't have another memorial service. I don't scatter ashes, because I did that already. The time for that is past, drifted away with the spring blossoms, the fading, falling lilac petals. Instead, your urn sits on my bookshelf, silent.

You don't talk to me so much these days. But I like having you there. It's comforting, in a way. Funny that, I like you better dead than I did alive. Funny how things work out sometimes. I head outside, cigarette pack and lighter in hand. I never could quite kick the habit. Don't think I ever will. And honestly, I'm not sure I want to. I've gotten a taste for it lately. It might break my heart someday, but then I already know how that feels.

Out in the garden, the leaves swirl autumn brown around my feet, the year turning. I breathe in, inhaling the smoke deep along with the cool air.

Your smile touches the corners of my mouth, and I know you're here. You'll always be here.

And I'm fine with that. We're joined.

It would break my heart to lose you.

RUBBLE PEOPLE
Matthew Sanborn Smith

The local Partyville starts to peel apart around us: the booth, the ball pit, a video game and the netting between them, the pizza on the table and the table too. Shards of pressboard and plastic fly toward me while molding themselves into the form of a man. A couple of the other moms scream and their kids run to them. I didn't expect this, but I know what it is.

"It's David!" I shout at them. "It's just David!" I look at Lainey, three years old today and so much tougher than the adults behind her. She's seen this before. Whatever party we might have had is in a shambles now. But I don't care. David's here.

"Look, honey, Daddy's accumulating!" I say.

When they see Lainey and me standing our ground, the others calm down a little, but Gina and Dara still scoop their kids up and head for the door, sprinkling f-words like holy water. Marie's backed into a corner with little Farrah in her arms. Farrah's tiny face is splotched pink and shiny wet. Her mouth hangs open. Marie's does the same. They're too afraid to come over, too curious to leave. I feel a little bad (because everybody kicked in for the party) but not too bad, because they're being stupid.

David has finally come together. "I wanted to see my little girl on her birthday," he says. I pick up Lainey and the two of us hug this weird conglomeration of a man. I kiss David's pepperoni lips, taste his grease with a flick of my tongue. The broad orange booth tabletop is his chest and its base is one of his legs. He's got plastic balls from the ball pit and a sound card voice box from a videogame. He kisses Lainey, who laughs and wipes her hand in the new grease on her face.

"It's so good to see you, baby," I tell him. It is good, but it takes all I have to not cry on him. I don't want to waste the little bit of time we have together by bringing him down. It's my job to hold everything up. I'm not doing my job very well.

"You too, babe," David says. "I only have a minute before they look in on me again."

"Daddy, it's my birfday!" Lainey says.

"I know it's your birthday, honey! That's why I'm here. Damn, you're gettin' big!"

Lainey sticks her hand into her father's face and tastes it.

"I'm sorry, David," I say.

"For what?" he asks in his chiptune voice.

"For having fun sometimes. For being happy. For smiling. I feel guilty when you're over there, fighting."

I can almost make out the memory of his cheekbones in his pizza crust face. He says, "But I want you to do all that, Beth. I want you to have a good life. That's what I'm fighting for. I want you to show this girl she can have a good life even if some other people can't."

"Which other people?" For a second I wonder if he's talking about his buddies' husbands and wives.

"The people over here. Or over there. You know what I mean. Where we're fighting." He means North Africa, he's just not allowed to say it.

The decision bursts out of me. I finally hit **[send]** on the projection unit in my head, but it isn't the courage that's been sitting there since I had it installed a few months ago that I pull out of myself. The transfer is P2P: psyche to psyche. The unit facilitates by making us hallucinate our own icons to manipulate. I feel a thick thread worming its way out of my left eyeball, one from my left nostril, one from my left ear. They weave themselves together and I yank at the cord. It feels like I've torn a piece of my brain out along with it. I don't think it was supposed to work like that.

I've reached in and taken out the impulses, the memories, the ghosts of the neural nets that make up my compassion and my caring. I force them on him, plastering the sticky thing to the table bolt that punctures the orange formica and forms David's nipple. And then it's a part of him as if it always had been.

He leans back for a moment, like I shoved him. "Oh," he says, surprised. His salt and pepper cap eyes leak salt and pepper tears.

"Jesus, you shouldn't have done that, baby. You know I can't give that back." He grabs me tight in his plywood arms, the hard materials of his body somehow feeling softer when he squeezes them into me. He feels warmer, that's for sure. But I care less.

"I had to do something," I say. "I need for something to change. I need you to change and me and this whole goddamned situation. I've had enough of this."

"Jesus, I'm sorry."

"It's not your fault. It's someone else's. I'm sorry. I'm doing this all wrong. I didn't mean to—"

"We'll do something," he says, and kisses us both. "We'll work this out. I gotta go now. I love you guys."

When he's gone, I sit in the wreckage of the booth, in the pile of junk that used to be a table and a lot of other things and also used to be my husband. Without the table to cover me, I can see my belly popping out from below the hem of my Goodbye Kitty T-shirt. White. Fat. Ugly. My outie gross as ever, like a curling pigtail that got squashed trying to escape.

The manager comes over. He says, "You're gonna have to pay for this."

I look him straight in the eye, not giving a fuck about him or what he wants. "Here," I say. I throw one of the balls from the ballpit at him. He takes it in his gut like it's a medicine ball. "You didn't have the balls to come over when my husband was here. See if you've got the balls to make me."

David remoted himself to the moon once. He didn't tell anyone but me. He doesn't think anyone else has ever done it. I look up at it sometimes, especially when it's full, and I think about him. Once, not long ago, a man made of moonrock walked on the surface up there, shuffling off gray dust. David might be the only one in the world who can go that far. I always knew he was special. He's incredible. And I'm lucky.

I couldn't even have kids before David. My parents died when I was young and I was sterilized at the orphanage. I met David before he enlisted and we talked about adopting. After he joined up, he found out a way to give me a maybe baby. It was a trick he learned in the army. On his second leave, he reached into me with that spirit part of himself, his radio flesh is what he calls it. While we were having sex, he reached into my womb and accumulated the tiniest part of me. He touched millions of cells. Chances were good one of them would be enough like an egg to take. It did. It wasn't enough like an egg to give me a completely healthy baby, but the doctors fixed that. I'm so grateful for Lainey.

David sneaks over sometimes, like at Partyville. He's not supposed to. He can get into a lot of trouble if he gets caught, but the minders turn the other way for a few minutes now and then. He figures they know that remotes need a little contact to keep from killing civilians outside of the designated war zonc. There have been too many incidents involving the Formosa Strait vets. The minders don't seem as bothered about the civilians inside the zone, though.

On our side, the Turks and the Ozzies get the worst of it because they use real people. Their soldiers are tanked up like Iron Man, flesh and blood inside. But really, the worst side to be on is no side. David never wants to talk about fighting, but once in a while, when he's saddest, he'll slip and mention the kids or the women or the old people. Then he just falls apart.

I hold him, whatever body he's in.

I'll have to remember the way I do that for next time, so it feels right to him and maybe he'll forget my emotional amputation. The mutilations underneath the skin are easier to hide. In the short term, anyway.

I wonder, if there are ever astronauts again, if they might find what looks like a shattered statue of a man while they're on the moon. They'd freak. I wonder if he could go to the sun. I wonder if someday people will kill each other in those places, too.

I can't fucking deal with this anymore. I shouldn't have to. I wipe Lainey's red, running nose and the snot pouring over her lip. I have to call out again because daycare won't take her sick. I'm gonna get fired, I know I am, and David doesn't make enough to keep us going by himself. I'm letting the month-overdue rent slide so I can make the month-overdue car payment. I can't drive the house, but we can sleep in the car.

Lainey's screaming and miserable. I hold her against my old Bruins sweatshirt, pat her back, step around the toys on the floor and into the fruit punch stains on the carpet. She won't go down to sleep. She's got a fever and even if I had the gas money to get to the walk-in clinic, I couldn't afford the co-pay. I put a cold washcloth on her forehead and give her a second Flintstone chewable. I don't know what else to do. A sick baby eats you.

Even though I gave David my compassion, I still know I'm supposed to feel for Lainey. I know I'm supposed to take care of her. I'm trying to do what a person who feels what they're supposed to feel would do. I'm doing what I think I would have done a week ago in this situation. It feels strange. I had the projection unit installed in my head months ago during the war drive at the recruitment center because it got us $30.00 a month more on our EBT chip. We could've gotten more if I actually used the damned thing the way the army wants me to.

With the civilian units, we can't remote like soldiers do, just project pieces of our personalities. We can't get back what we send like soldiers do. I chickened out before the first send. What I projected into David at Partyville was the first emotion I ever gave away.

The army wants our determination, our positive attitudes. They want our courage. I'm afraid to give my courage. The ones who gave it wound up giving more than they expected. I'd seen other people, David's dad for one, give his courage for the war drive and then live in fear about everything that came down. He gave away his car, thinking it was a deathtrap. He gave away his sleep and can hardly function anymore.

I wish there was someone I could give my worry to. I wish there was someone I could give my fear to. This poverty. No one wants any of it. Not even the enemy would be stupid enough to take it.

I find twelve dollars in an envelope I was supposed to pay back to Gina, but I didn't see Gina on Tuesday like I was supposed to. She's being a bitch, still freaked out over David showing up at Partyville. But I'm glad she's being a bitch because twelve dollars is something. Add that to the money I scrape up from behind the crumb-covered cushions, from the sticky cup holder in the car, from the bottom of my pocketbook, from Lainey's glass penny jar, and I come up with fifteen dollars and thirty-eight cents. I can find something for Lainey in the cold and flu aisle at Sav-A-Lot for fifteen dollars and thirty-eight cents. I know I can. I have to.

In the store, Lainey's griping on my shoulder. She wants to be held everywhere we go. The most expensive stuff, anywhere in the store, is always on the shelf at eye level. I don't even know what's up there anymore. My eyes automatically go to the bottom shelf. I've been shopping the bottom shelf for a year and a half.

The cheapest thing they have is $16.99, a tiny bottle of some generic cherry-flavored cough syrup. It's made for adults. I read the bottle again. It says not to be taken by children under twelve, but it doesn't say why. Maybe if I just give her a quarter of a teaspoon, it'll knock her out. I pace the speckled tiles of the cold and flu aisle with Aaron Neville singing overhead on the PA system and I wonder if the cough syrup would hurt her. And if I decide it won't, how do I come up with three more dollars? Lainey screams in my ear and I look for a woman, because a mother should understand.

Two aisles over, it's a woman with dyed brown hair and curls the size of soup cans. She's in a long fuzzy coat, pushing a cart, and checking out the corn pads. "Ma'am, could you help me, please? My baby's sick and I just need three more dollars to get her some medicine."

She sighs, a little huffy, but there's no denying Lainey's a restless mess. She goes into her pocketbook, and I don't care if it's a hassle for her. I'm closer every minute to doing whatever it takes to get by. The world has kicked me around enough.

"Hold up!" comes a voice from behind me. I turn and see

Gianni in his Sav-A-Lot vest. Shit. Gianni, the most vile human being I know, is out on the sales floor.

Gianni couldn't get into the army. Psychic deformity. He couldn't accumulate, couldn't function even in a supporting role, much less combat. He felt guilt over that. Dara said he tried to kill himself. Ran his electric car in the garage hoping to die from carbon monoxide poisoning. We used to call psychic deformity "stupid" when I was little. Now he's a fucking disaster with a name tag.

"Ma'am, please put your money away. I apologize. We have rules against begging." His finger's in my face. "You're coming back to the office," he says to me.

Idiot Gianni grabs the arm I'm holding Lainey with and she almost tumbles to the floor. The lady says, "Oh!" and reaches her hands toward her. I catch Lainey with my other arm, the one that was waiting for those three dollars.

"What the fuck, Gianni! You almost made me drop her!"

I jerk the arm he has upward to hit him in the face but he pulls back and I only catch the end of his nose. He slams his open hand into my head and I knock skulls with Lainey.

"Hey, stop it!" The lady screams. Her hands are up, half to grab at us, and half to stop any fists flying at her. Lainey is outright crying.

"What the hell is going on here?" Gianni's boss, big Steve Arden, is pulling Gianni off of me. I know it's smart to pull back and act innocent, but I can't help kicking him in the leg while he's still in reach. Gianni spits at me and lands one on my hoodie while a couple of other stock boys run in and try to hold his swinging arms. He's crying too, and screaming incoherently.

"He hit her!" the lady says.

"I'm so sorry, Beth," Steve says to me, "You know the situation with Gianni."

Yeah, I know the situation. Gianni gave his courage to the war drive and he gave his determination. He gave his good citizenship, he gave his driving skills, his rock-skipping ability, his knowledge of boiling water. He gave everything they would let him give because he wanted to give something. He wanted to give everything, but they don't want all of it, only the good things. He's left with everything that makes him human trash, all the shit no one would ever want, with the guilt that sold off everything else sitting right there on the top of the pile.

He can't even be the greeter at the Sav-A-Lot. But Steve, who went to school with David's cousin, can't fire Gianni. Says the government won't let him. Gianni's a war hero as far as they're concerned, even though he's never fired a shot. Or maybe part of him has now. Steve has to give him at least four hours a week.

"I don't care what the situation is," I say to Steve, "That's assault and I want you to call the cops on him."

Steve stands a little taller, like he hadn't thought of that. "I'll be more than happy to do that. Don't you worry about a thing. Do you need to see a doctor?"

My mind races. "Lainey does. Gianni knocked my head into hers. She might have a concussion." I hope Steve doesn't think about it too hard and question if Lainey can even get a concussion. No, he's rattled, thank God. If not because of us, then because of this lady.

"All right, let me call 911, we'll fix this whole thing up. Are you all right, Ma'am?" he asks the lady.

"I'm fine. You need to fire that maniac."

"I hope I can, Ma'am."

"Thank you, Steve," I say.

I never would have guessed Gianni would be the best thing that happened to me today.

David says the locals have different names for remote soldiers depending on where they're fighting. When they see action in the desert, they call them sand devils. In the cities they're called rubble people. I think about rubble people every time I give Lainey another vitamin: Barney, Betty, Bamm-Bamm. I think about David accumulating in the vitamin factory, a man made of sweet pastel chalk. I like to imagine that Lainey would get better if she could take a big bite of him like that.

He says he can feel himself while he moves between bodies. His buddies say he's imagining it. They travel at light speed from human body to accumulated body and back. They say there's not enough time to feel anything in between. He says he takes his time and feels it and I believe him. The only thing that keeps the others from trying it is fear. The fear of not being able to get back to their bodies.

But anything can be our bodies. The whole world can be our body. I think I want to do it, be out of my body. But for longer than a microsecond. I want to fly without any weight, knowing I could never be heavy enough to fall.

When our men and women come home, our boys and girls, the ones that are still alive aren't only human. They've collected pieces of the world inside them and become unrefined, like metal being turned back to ore. A remote might go out and become a tree walker in Indonesia, a jungle soldier made of vines and unlucky monkeys. And when she comes back to the base, a tiny bit of her real body changes. Maybe a few cells of a blood vessel wall turn to sap. And maybe she wonders where that bruise came from and how much of her is still her. This is the first war where wounds can add to a soldier's weight instead of take away. They wear their tree bark skin, their concrete joints, their iron wounds, and they like to think they're stronger for it.

I wonder what David's going to bring back inside himself. And what he might leave behind.

Lainey's been deleted.

I can't understand this. I can't believe this. I keep going over it to remind myself that it really has happened. My life hasn't quite synced with reality, I guess.

Her eyes look like something from a taxidermist's sample, only soft. I can still see them through the steel door. She looked like she was getting better since the emergency room. They gave her antibiotics, the fever seemed to be easing up. Then this morning she stopped.

I can't afford the emergency room like Sav-A-Lot can. I call the doctor who grew the brain she shouldn't have been born with. He says that in Poland there was a baby like Lainey who had a fever. Her brain overclocked and it wiped her mind clear.

I ask him, "Could Lainey's mind have gone somewhere else, like her father's does when he's remote?"

"There's been no evidence to show that's the case," the doctor says. He sounds the same way I remember him. Gentle. Smart.

"Can you make another brain like her last one?"

"We can actually salvage the brain she already has. That wouldn't be the issue. The problem is we can't get her memories back. She'd be mentally like a newborn and the new connections and memories that formed in her brain would mean she'd be a different person, not the Lainey you knew. On top of that, I'm afraid Medicaid wouldn't cover the procedure."

"If I could find Lanie's memories online or if her father can find them in North Africa, could you put them back?" The words sound crazier outside of my head than inside. His sigh rolls through the connection like a thick, tired fog.

"I think the best thing for you in this moment is to get some rest. I'm very sorry for your loss."

There are no police. There's no medical examiner, there's no funeral home. As far as the law is concerned, Lainey was stillborn three years ago. I don't have the heart to bury my own little girl. I don't want her waking up trapped in a box under a ton of earth. I didn't know what else to do. Her body's in the kitchen freezer.

I press my face against the freezer door. I can't ever open it again. On the counter are the freezer shelf and the ice cube trays and a box of frozen peas and my favorite flavor of melting ice cream. My face is hot and swollen and wet. I'm babbling. Telling her things I'd planned to tell her when she was older. I'm not supposed to shake like this, am I? I'm not supposed to feel as much pain as I do. I guess compassion isn't exactly love. It isn't exactly that feeling you have when another person was your whole life, sick and all.

"Daddy went through me once, with his radio flesh," I tell Lainey with my hand balling up against the door. I don't want her to be lonely in there. "That's how we made you. You were a miracle. Three years is more than I ever should have had with you, baby, and I'm so, so grateful for that. But am I greedy for wanting even more?"

There's nothing else to be done, but I keep standing here because what the hell else can I do? I haven't made a move in years that wasn't based around Lainey. Would I have tried harder if she was a real baby? I mean, she is a real baby. Was a real baby. Is there some maternal instinct I never got because she wasn't completely natural? Is there some part of me that would have done anything to recover her, even whored for the money, if she was like all the other kids? Is that the part I gave to David on Lainey's birthday?

34

For the first time ever, I hope David doesn't visit me. I can't be the one to tell him that his daughter is dead. He's going to blame me. I know he's going to blame me. I can't face that. I can't ever face him again. My whole life is fucked. It's all fucked. I think it always was. I was just too stupid to see it.

My eyes are burning. My face and the kitchen floor are wet. I have to get out. We used to go out all the time when David was here. We had more money then. I can't believe how many better days there used to be. I'm home more now. I have to go somewhere to just get away from the apartment and my life. To get away from the freezer.

I'm sorry, David. I didn't have what it takes to hold it together. I know I should admit I failed as a mother and as a wife and as a person, but, fuck, I'm sure I didn't fail. It was the world that failed me.

There are two ways this can go. Either way, it's the end. The one way, I can crumble. But I don't have what it takes to kill myself. I don't want to die, anyway. I want everything else to die. That's the other way. I can scratch at the eyes of God.

I'm going to go down to Second Street where the homeless lady with the cardboard sign hangs out on the corner and I'm going to give it all away to her, everything left that's good about me, just like Gianni did. Either Gianni is a real person and Lainey was a real baby and I was a real mother or none of that is true. I don't know which. I don't know if it matters and I think I don't care. I'm going to give myself away to the woman, give her everything about me that was ever any good. Except whatever murderous courage might still be in me.

The world will get whatever's left of me. The darkness, the destruction, the cruelty and the cowardice. It'll get what it deserves. The world declared war on me when I was eleven years old. My forces have been deteriorating ever since. This malformed society has whittled me down to a single atom and taken one last swipe at it. That atom is about to explode. I'm going to make this corner of America my very own North Africa.

I hope when David is a very old man and finally passes, they open him and are shocked to see a little sprinkling of moon dust inside of him. I hope that his radio flesh will still be alive there on the moon, young and unburdened by his rubble flesh here. I hope Lainey's there waiting for him and they live long, happy lives far away from this place.

I go outside to the car and leave the front door of the apartment wide open. I'm going to find my next body.

DESERT STAND
Richard C. Rogers

Be strong. Be quick and alive, or be dead...

Out here in the white sky and heat and dust, in the endless crush of days killed with booze, tobacco, and troubled sleep, a man can flatten in a hurry. When Death comes calling he'll simply hold out his hands and say "Cuff me, Death. I'm tired."

For six months I've been hiding out here in the big nowhere. Twice I'd made my stand in brighter places–places with fine hotels, fine women, and fine liquor. But Mallory's got long arms, and eyes in many cities. The first time his men came after me, I spotted them before they saw me and lit out. The second time they surprised me at night. I nearly bought it then–it led to a horse-doctor carving two slugs from my arm without anesthetic. The scars on my sunburned flesh are white as teeth.

That was the end of the bright lights for me. I fled south and rented a shack at the end of a dirt road, half a dozen miles from the nearest village. The first month I just sat around and smoked, watched buzzards whirl in the flat sky until sundown, then drank myself to sleep. When I woke up one morning and felt exhausted putting on my shoes, I knew I was going soft fast. Same as I knew Mallory wasn't done with me.

I'm a stubborn fool. I was sick of running, sick of hiding, sick of living, but I still didn't want to make it easy for him, so I resolved that morning to get back in shape.

Two miles from my shack a mesa rises from the plain. A steep climb brings you to a vista where you can see for miles in every direction. Far to the north is the American border. Off to the west the blue Pacific gleams. East, a trail leads down to a desert studded with dust devils and cacti.

I've been making this hike every day for five months. East is always the direction I end up looking. East to nothing. It has a hold on me I can't explain. Once I'd followed that downward trail–I don't know why. Curiosity, maybe. A mile in I felt as lost and alone as a man can be. The bleached white deadliness of it fascinated me. It was like being on another planet. Each step became harder. The hot air seared my lungs. There was nothing out there for me. Nothing to go back to. My canteen was empty and it occurred to me to keep walking–to go out into the emptiness and die. You can't get more lost than that. And the running would be over.

But I finally turned around and headed back…

The thought came again. *Be strong. Be quick and alive, or be dead…*

Not much choice really. I threw my cigarette onto the rocks, watched it burn away, then started towards home. As I crossed the ridge overlooking my shack I spotted a flash of chrome by the side of the road, and dropped down between the rocks.

Three at least, I figured. It had been three last time.

They'd have come up on the house en masse at first. But what was their move when they found it empty? If it was me, I'd place one man inside, one back at the car in case the quarry snuck in behind and tried to jack it, and one on high ground, covering the other two.

That was the man I needed to take care of first.

I searched every crevice with my eyes, every place a man with a rifle might hide. He was easy to spot. Mallory had sent city men, and the idiot in the rocks was wearing a blue shirt.

Belly to the ground, I started crawling.

One wrong move, that's all it takes. Where had I made mine?

Then I knew…

Three days ago, late in the morning when I was sleeping one off, a racket outside woke me up. I grabbed my gun from under the pillow and went to the door. The dirt road outside my shack ends in a cul-de-sac, and I saw some fool kid circling around out there on a rusty old bike with a bell on it. He wore a stupid lopsided grin and was banging that bell like it was Christmas.

"Hey!" I yelled. "Shut up!" The little twerp smiled at me and kept hitting the bell.

As I crossed the yard I could tell there was something wrong with him, something off in his head. He was a good-looking kid, too, with shiny black eyes and a mop of black hair. It was sad. At the same time, his loopy smile was infectious, and I smiled back.

That made him giggle and bang the bell even harder.

"You want to maybe stop doing that?" I said. Stupid question. I said it in English, for one thing, but even if I used Spanish I doubt he'd have understood me. He stopped banging the bell, though, when he saw the nickel-plated automatic sticking from the waistband of my pants. Laughing up a storm, he reached out and practically fell off his bike. I caught him just in time. He looked at me with wide eyes and grabbed for my gun again.

"Hold on," I said, catching his hand. "That's not a toy."

Man, that kid could laugh. That's about all he did.

"Go home now, fella," I said as gently as I could. Something in my tone must have reached him, because his face went dark and sad. He hit the bell again, dispiritedly this time. It made me feel awful.

Hell. Sleep was gone anyway. I went inside, brewed coffee, and pulled a coke from the icebox. When I returned, the boy was staring off across the road at a yellow butterfly. I handed him the coke and he drank it in three gulps, spilling most of it over his chin and down his shirtfront. He watched me every second as I sipped my coffee, like he was fascinated. I was the morning show.

When my coffee was gone he yanked a baseball from his pocket and held it out. It was a sad affair. It looked like a dog had been chewing on it. The kid dropped his bike to the ground and ran off a short distance, then stuck out his hands.

Shoot. I soft-tossed him the ball. The kid lit up when he caught it, and threw it back. Well, halfway back. It rolled in the dust.

The weirdest game of catch followed. He could catch all right, but his throws were way off. I could see him straining each time to concentrate, but when he released there was no telling where the ball would go. I tired out before he did, and called the game off.

"We oughta be getting you home, son. I imagine your folks are worried about you." He stared at me, so I walked back up the road a bit, then waved for him to follow. He wobbled onto his bike and set off beside me.

It was a mile to the nearest house. There was a shade tree out front, and cultivated fields behind. I saw a Mexican working out there.

"Hello!" I called.

The man raised his head, no doubt wondering what a gringo was doing in his front yard. He walked towards me, his scythe gripped in one fist. With his face hidden under a sombrero, I could just see his chin jutting out, and the slash of his mouth.

"This your boy?" I said, when he was twenty yards away.

He removed his hat and wiped his forehead. "Ah. Sí, sí. Gracias."

I saw his face then, saw weariness and sadness in his eyes as he moved up to the boy and tousled his hair. The kid giggled. What a surprise.

"All right then," I said. "Adiós." I turned on my heel.

"Señor," the man said, gesturing me to wait. He disappeared inside, returning with two cold Tecates, and handed me one. "Por favor."

"Thanks," I said. I pulled out my cigarettes, took one for myself, then held out the pack.

"Sí. Gracias."

We squatted under the shade tree, smoking and drinking without saying anything. At one point I noticed we were both watching the boy, off running in the pepper field. He was the liveliest thing going.

"Nice kid," I said.

Despite his sad eyes, the man smiled and nodded.

When our cigarettes were finished I thanked him for the beer, then set out for home. As I walked down the road I felt eyes on my back. I glanced behind and saw the boy, standing stock still, watching me go.

That night I sat up, thinking. When dawn rolled out I walked into town. The shops there were pretty basic. I couldn't find what I wanted so I caught the bus into Acapulco. Man, it felt good to feel that cool ocean breeze again, to see fine women in sleek dresses.

I found what I needed in a big tourist shop, then checked into a beachfront hotel, asking for their best suite. After showering I went downstairs for dinner and drinks. The liquor did what it does. I got that jumpy feeling, of things out in the night waiting to be discovered. After eating I found a casino and played blackjack for a couple hours, dropping a few hundred. I didn't care–I liked the action. And the women. I didn't have time to do the wining and dining bullshit, so after cashing out I found a helpful cabbie who drove me to a place where I could buy one.

That night I slept like a lord on clean sheets. In the morning I felt so good I thought about staying on another night, but I didn't want to press my luck, so after breakfast I took the bus back to nowhere.

Walking home, I passed the boy's house. Nobody was around. I dropped two brand new baseball gloves and three shiny baseballs on the porch. Maybe they'd make the kid happy. I mean, he seemed happy, in his lost way. But who knows what it's really like to live inside such a mind?

Back home my place seemed more desolate than usual. After a dinner of corned beef hash I took a bottle of Irish to the porch and sat drinking as night came on.

The next day I couldn't shake a feeling of unease. The silence felt heavy. The sound of wind got on my nerves. That night I drank myself blind, and when I staggered to bed I fell into a swift nightmare of Diablo's face moving towards me in the dark. In the morning I felt half-dead, but still jittery, so I hoofed it to the mesa, trying to walk off my unease…

All this went through my mind as I worked down the slope. They must have spotted me in Acapulco. Mallory moved fast, and now his men waited below while my piece was back home.

As I squirmed along, I worked loose a rock the size of my fist. About twenty yards away I began to smell the man in the rocks. Cheap aftershave. Tobacco. Fear.

At the last second, too late, he turned and saw me. My first blow broke his skull. Shit exploded from his ass as he died. Christ.

I grabbed the dead man's carbine and rolled away, spitting bile from my mouth, then moved on to the second man. He died chomping a cigar in the front seat of a Buick, shot through the head at fifty yards.

Armed with carbine and pistol, I hurried down the side of the road, moving from cover to cover. Fifty yards from the shack I pulled up behind a boulder. "You inside!" I shouted. "We can make this easy or make it hard. Your partners are dead. You can walk out of here with your life and we'll call it a day. Your move!"

Silence.

"You really want to die for Mallory?" I yelled.

A fusillade followed. Bullets pinged off the boulder. I had my answer–only one gunman remained. I flung a shot his way, shattering a window, then ducked down at his answering volley. *Go on*, I thought. *Waste your bullets.*

The sun beat down on my face from the white sky. High above, buzzards circled, coming for the feast. It was a waiting game now. Waiting in the wind and silence…

The faint sound of a bell reached me. Back along the road, the kid rode into view, peddling his bike like a fiend. I couldn't make out his face at the distance, but I knew he was smiling and giggling.

"Go on back!" I yelled.

At the sound of my voice the kid redoubled his efforts. I looked across the road, spotting my next cover. When the kid was just about on me I jumped up, fired two shots at the house, then sprinted for him, planning to snatch him up and make a dive for the opposite side. As I grabbed him a bullet tugged my shirt. I spun and emptied a full magazine at the dim figure in the doorway. My shots kicked the fool back into the dark. I ran up, carbine out, but it was over. He'd already bled out on the floor.

I rushed back to the kid.

He was gone, lying in the dusty road like something thrown away. A shiny new ball stuck from his shirt pocket. The two baseball gloves hung from the back of his bike.

I carried him to the shade of the porch and washed the blood from his face, trying not to look at the bullet hole, but it grew and grew until it felt like it was swallowing me. My eyes went wet. I looked up at the white sky, saw Diablo rearing high on his bloody steed, roaring with laughter at this death and waste.

I thought about the Buick up the road. I could take it and head south, find a new place to hide. Sure…

But who'd die next time?

Inside the house I worked loose the floorboards in the corner and pulled out the suitcase. Something like two hundred grand remained. Not enough. Nothing could be enough.

I picked the boy up. He weighed hardly anything.

Back at his house I spied his father out in the fields. Keeping low, I carried the boy to the foot of the shade tree and laid him there with the suitcase beside him. I moved a strand of hair from his eyes, then hurried away.

Atop the mesa I can see for miles in every direction. Behind me a trail leads back to the world–before me a trail leads down to the desert. My mistake last time had been in turning back. I won't make that mistake again.

I open my canteen and throw it to the ground. As the sand drinks its water, I move forward…

E HYDERABAADUS
Megan Chaudhuri

It's barely dawn and already I've sweated through my cotton dress, but Conchi doesn't say anything as she helps me sit at my workbench. Hazy gray light slants through my shop's front window, reflecting off the diagnostic laptop and the gutted phone I was repairing yesterday. The light diffracts like a prism through vials of antiseptic ethanol and freeze-dried virus kept nearby–just in case. I never forget *los Días de Silencio*.

Behind me, I hear Conchi fiddling with the air conditioner. Blessed, costly coolness flows over my bare legs.

"Not today," I say, lifting up my wig to mop my neck. At least my makeup's not running. "It's cloudy. Power's going to cost too much."

"Elena." Conchi's Mayan accent is stronger than usual. "It will be thirty-eight degrees today. Your heart–"

"–will be fine," I interrupt, climbing down from the stool, "until I see what your fiancé charges me for draining his reserve batteries dry." Holding onto the workbench, I slap the power button. The air conditioner whines down.

Conchi says nothing, her back still to me. In the silence between us, Ticulito flows in through the open door: the hum of the weekly Ticul bus charging at the depot; the gobble of turkeys from nearby Mayan neighborhoods; the flat bass of a phone's speakers–probably a 2052 Pharaoh–blasting BBC Spanish from the laundry next door.

"You can afford it," Conchi whispers.

I halt on my way back to the stool.

"What?"

"You can afford it." Conchi whirls around, eyes wide. "And you can afford to pay me more after seven goddamn years–"

The words cut off as her hand flies to her mouth.

I sit stiffly and fiddle with the diagnostic probe, conscious of Conchi watching me with wide eyes. Sweat trickles down my back, as itching and uncomfortable as my thoughts: by Californian standards, I'm working poor. By Yucatan standards, I should be napping on a Cozumel beach, instead of working as a smartphone *mecánica* in the not-quite-slum of provincial Ticulito.

By either standard, I'm getting a helluva good deal paying local wages for Conchi to bathe, care for, and translate for me–on top of the repair work she does for my shop.

"*Concepción.*" My weak mouth muscles garble her full name. "You know I must save money for when I–"

"Pa'atiki'?" interrupts a young man's voice in Mayan.

He's barely in his teens, dressed in jeans and a faded *fútbol* jersey, helping an elderly woman into my shop. They're probably waiting for the bus to charge; I don't recognize either of them.

But I recognize the familiar look of someone choosing which of us to address: tall young Conchi, brown-skinned and bright-eyed, her face radiating intelligence, competence, and good genetic health.

Or me. One and a half meters, thickset, my fingers stubby and my face a flat moon that neither plastic surgery, makeup, nor a wig can quite hide. I'm a genetic mosaic–after the treatment in utero, only half my cells express the extra twenty-first chromosome–but I still look, move, and sound like someone with *Síndrome de Down*.

And, despite most of my brain's neurons, astrocytes, and microglia being genetically sound, I still have the same clinical fate.

The teen turns to the flustered Conchi. "Ma'lob ja'atskab…"

With some prompting, the elderly woman produces a smartphone. But she won't let her grandson hand it to Conchi; her expression is confused.

Demented. I wipe non-existent dirt off the virus vials, grasping for how to explain to Conchi that I can't pay her more without losing her entirely.

The conversation stops when Conchi coaxes the phone from the woman. Plastic crinkles as she puts it into a Ziploc bag. There's the click-rasp of a phone chassis being opened, then Conchi inhales sharply.

I look up. "What is it?"

The teen looks surprised that I talk.

"He says"–Conchi hands me the bagged phone–" his grandmother bought it months ago from the new reseller, but it doesn't work now even though they bought a replacement battery from a bodega. The reseller won't take it back after so long."

The new reseller. A Honduran refugee; his shop's a kilometer down the street. Nothing to Conchi, but practically back in Sacramento to me.

I turn over the phone. The chassis is new, but the insides are old Bionanite, the chips and wiring tangled into an organic-like mass from years of enzymatic self-repair.

In the morning light, the phone's guts look oddly shadowed. I shift the bag and a faint sulfurous scent puffs out in the split-second before I block the hole. The scent's as horribly familiar horribly familiar as the black specks of bacterial colonies now visible on the carbon nanotube scaffolding for the repair enzymes.

My eyes almost meet Conchi's.

E. hyderabaadus.

The most brilliant organism designed for degrading electronic waste. Until it bred with wildtype *E. coli* strains.

E. hyderabaadus. I remember the heavy quiet of the streets, the silence of Sacramento's skies, the sensation of a civilization holding its breath in *los Días de Silencio* after the bacteria reached America's phones–our ultralightweight, self-repairing phones.

"*E. hyderabaadus*," Conchi whispers. I nod, mind racing: for an infection this bad, I should dry-autoclave the phone and coat its guts with fresh enzyme-functionalized nanotubes. But older phones aren't built for autoclaving–and the new, heat-tolerant ones are clearly too expensive for this woman.

I look at my vials of bacteriophage virus. I'll have to kill *E. hyderabaadus* the biological way before I can re-coat it with fresh enzyme.

But I only have so many vials–and too many clients with old, vulnerable phones, out here in isolated Ticulito.

"Oh, shit," I say in English.

The reseller's shop is wedged between a private home and a stucco building, hidden behind a concrete wall with one of Ticulito's ubiquitous, hand-lettered signs. I lean against the concrete to catch my breath, feeling its heat radiate through my hand. My heart's doing one-fifty beats a minute but I resist the urge to call Conchi. Silence had coagulated between us, hard as a scab, after the teen and grandmother left with promises to recover the phone during Friday's market.

I pay Conchi the local wages for both an apprentice *mecánica* and health aide, I think, breathing hard. She'll have a bright, long future when I'm gone.

When my heart slows some, I stand up but my dress catches on the splintered edge of the sign. When I turn towards it the words "Pirvate Nursing Home: Dementia patients welcome!" leap at me. My fingers fumble and the cotton rips on the splinters.

"Shit." I shove the hole under my belt and check my pockets to make sure the sample wipes didn't fall out. Averting my face from the sign and the nursing home, I march into the reseller's.

It's so cold–so unexpected–that I gasp. Halogen bulbs radiate a silver-blue light that reflects off sterilizable phones– better than what most of Ticulito can afford–displayed on shelves. A nicely-dressed couple browse, their conversation melding with the whine of air conditioning and thump of Honduran techno.

My mouth falls open as a handsome man comes around the counter. My hands, grasping the sample wipes hidden in my pockets, go slack.

"Good morning, ma'am," he says in a deep voice with a pleasant accent. "I'm Domingo; welcome to my shop."

"Uh." Where is the hut crammed with ancient electronics? Where is the scrawny Honduran war refugee, the one who knows nothing about the risk of E. hyderabaadus bacteria contaminating old devices full of carbon nanotubes?

I realize he's looking at me, a little puzzled. I shut my mouth and mentally practice my speech exercises.

"Thank you, Domingo," I say. "Good morning to you, too." Standing up straight, I look about with what I hope is an expression of keen intelligence. It's so much worse when attractive men conclude that I'm retarded.

To my relief, he smiles. "Looking for anything specific?"

I shake my head. "Are you, um, the only Honduran reseller in this neighborhood?" My accent's really strong because I'm paying too much attention to how I speak; but I would prefer he thinks me a clueless rich gringo than anything else.

49

He nods. "So far as I know, ma'am. Where are you from?"

"Um," I say, approaching the shelves, feeling hyper-conscious of my loose-jointed walk. Guess he's it.

"California, originally," I say, brushing my forefinger over the square edges of a business model Caballo, my middle finger along the solid curves of an iPhone, my pinkie across the cold bulk of a customizable Pharaoh. "But I've lived here for twelve years now." Far, far away from my mother. You'd think a neuroscience professor who paid out of pocket for Down's genetic ablation–who paid for my Bachelor's at UCSF–would know better than to treat her middle-aged daughter like an idiot child.

"Really," he says, all politeness. The couple continue browsing, indifferent to just another foreigner.

When Domingo takes my shoulder I jerk with surprise. "Perhaps you'd be interested in Caballo's consumer release from last fall?"

His hand is warm as he leads me towards a shelf by the counter. Glass protects these high-end phones, and I look at his reflection instead of the display. He's well-built, muscular like a *fútbol* player. Even taller than Conchi.

If Conchi was here, he'd only be paying attention to her.

And who could blame him, I think as I catch my own reflection; at best, I hope to look like a profoundly unattractive woman with a heavy hand for makeup. Plus, the warm hand on my shoulder has a wedding band.

I pull my shoulder free. "Actually," I say, "I'm here about your bargain phones."

One black eyebrow arches. "Why? I'm certain, ma'am, that you can afford–"

"Well, actually," I interrupt, his words uncomfortably echoing what Conchi blurted earlier. My eyes settle on a framed printout behind him, showing an attractive woman with two children who resemble Domingo, posed in front of the iconic Cathedral of Co-mayagua.

Comayagua was fire-bombed last spring.

"I'm a *mecánica*, and I had two Mayan clients, um, bring in an old, non-autoclavable phone that was infected with *E. hyderabaadus*. They said they'd bought it from you several months ago."

The couple are staring at us now. Sweat breaks out beneath my wig. His expression grows stony.

"These are my wares," he says, gesturing at the phones glinting under the halogen lights. "And these are my customers." His hand sweeps towards the well-dressed couple with pale, almost *gringo* skin. "Perhaps there was a…misunderstanding."

I shift uncomfortably, understanding his implication. Most of the Honduran refugees fled north after the civil war started, but those who came to the Yucatan have clashed with locals competing for work. Locals like Mayan *nativos*.

"Um," I say, conscious of how the couple stare at me, how my wig needs to be adjusted and my dress sewn where I tore it and that I'm starting to slouch and drop my chin and speak weird. "Perhaps. But–just remembered the outbreak there is to you, okay?" I finish, stumbling over my Spanish conjugations for the first time in years.

I bite my lip, hard. Language breakdown is one of the symptoms. Has it started?

He nods and moves past me. Humid air laps against my legs; he is holding the door open.

"Thank you," I mutter, walking past him with my loose-hipped, hitching stride. The warmth swallows me and I keep my face averted from his, my eyes averted from the sign waiting for me: "Private Nursing Home: Dementia patients welcome!"

Money. I wrap the thought around me like my mother's overprotective hug. Thank God for my money; when it comes for me (is it coming already?), I'll be able to afford a high-end nursing home in Ticul, instead of one of these rundown places dotting Ticulito.

I'm halfway back before I remember. Pulling the sample wipes out of my pocket, I rub a different one over each of my short fingers and then my shoulder, where Domingo touched me. Then, my fists tight, I shuffle back to my store.

The next morning I'm at my workbench, processing the sample wipes from Domingo's store and the other bodegas selling old phones, when my second-least-favorite person walks in like he owns the place.

"Felipe!" Conchi says. Setting down the screwdriver, she embraces the tall young Mayan man in too-fashionable clothes.

I wrinkle my nose as cologne and the faint ozone of warm solar panels waft towards me, followed by Felipe and Conchi.

"Hello, Felipe," I say, my words stiffer than usual. Keeping my eyes on my work, I stopper the small glass vials full of sample wipes and bright pink phenol-chloroform.

"Ba'ax ka wa'alik, Miss Elena," he says.

"'Hello,'" Conchi translates.

"I gleaned that, thank you," I snap. Felipe's grin fades; he knows Spanish. "Conchi?"

She drops Felipe's arm. The glass vials clink as she snaps them into a plastic rack. When she shakes it, the phenol-chloroform turns opaque and bubbly, leaching out the DNA and junk proteins from the wipes.

Felipe watches her. I watch him, impatient for him to stop flirting and leave.

In lightly-accented Spanish, he says, "What are you doing, Conchi?"

"She's isolating DNA from the samples we took," I say quickly, "so we can test for traces of *E. hyderabaadus*." Holding the workbench for balance, I lean across and slap the smeared touch screen of the boxy little nanoarray reader I got secondhand from a retired professor. The screen lights up. "There's been an outbreak, and we need to locate the source."

Felipe looks at me, then fires questions in Mayan at Conchi while she loads the vials into our small centrifuge.

My teeth are gritting. I focus on parameterizing the screening protocol on the nanoarray. Normally, I tolerate Felipe well enough; he makes Conchi happy, even though I always have to negotiate down my electricity bill with him. But right now he's making me extra jumpy and irritable.

No–I've been jumpy and irritable since Domingo's store yesterday. Since I walked past the dementia home.

"Is that why my new phone isn't working?" Felipe suddenly says in Spanish. He sounds worried–and should be, because out here in Ticulito, some older solar panels still have nanotubes.

Conchi and I both turn towards Felipe, neither of us looking at each other.

"What?"

"My new phone." Felipe takes out last fall's Caballo Pro, all chrome and gold. "I bought it from that new Honduran place yesterday and it stopped working this morning."

"But the bacteria take months to grow–" Conchi snatches it from him.

"He could've put a new chassis over old electronics," I say.

Conchi nods. Picking up a plastic bag, she wraps it around the phone. I hear the click-rasp of the phone coming apart.

And then Conchi's snort.

"What is it?" I say.

She brings it over, tossing aside the bag. "The solder's loose on a battery connection." She solicitously tilts it so I can see the tiny battery, so new there's no signs of self-repair. I just as solicitously look; we're still doing this awkward dance around the elephant in the room, the elephant Conchi pointed at yesterday.

"No bacteria?" Felipe says.

"Of course there are bacteria." I set the phone down. "Just not the ones we're concerned about."

Conchi unloads the samples. Centrifugation has squished each wipe to the tube's bottom, separated the phenol-chloroform by density into layers: pink on bottom, thick with proteins, and translucent phenol above, full of DNA.

"You fix the phone," I say, trading the phone for the samples.

As I pipet the DNA into the nanoarray, Felipe starts drumming his fingers and talking in rapid Mayan.

Conchi replies in Spanish. The solder gun clicks on and I smell hot metal as she cements the wire back in place. They go back and forth, Conchi slipping into Mayan, getting louder and louder, Felipe drumming his fingers more and more quickly–

Felipe jerks when I slap his hand.

"Stop that, goddammit," I say, tasting the bile of long-simmered irritation.

"You," he says. Surprised, I look up into his finger in my face. "Find out who's selling contaminated phones. They're putting my solar panels at risk."

"You're not the only one at risk," I snap. I don't like having a finger in my face; it's too much like pointing. Pointing at the weird girl. I had enough of that back on Sacramento playgrounds.

The solder gun clicks off.

Felipe takes the phone from her. "Dios bo'otik..." he says, continuing in a long, angry burst. I hear my name several times and, in Spanish, the words 'rich *gringo*.'

"Jesus Christ." I deliberately look down at my samples. My hands shake a little as I finish loading them. Felipe finally shuts up and turns away, but I don't speak until I hear his dress shoes hit the pavement outside. "What was all that about, Conchi?"

She's quiet so long that I turn towards her, one hand holding the workbench, the other hovering above the touch screen. Her back is to me.

"Conchi?"

She turns, her symmetrical face–every feature proportional and healthy–expressionless. "He says, figure out who it is, and he'll cut their power off and drive them out."

"Why'd he keep saying my name?"

Next door, someone changes the station; there's a burst of muffled Honduran techno.

"He thinks you…" she hesitates, shoulders hunched. "He thinks you are fine with someone selling infected phones, because it brings you more business."

I turn sharply back to the nanoarray reader. "That's nonsense," I say. Even though it's bringing me business now, there's no way I could keep on top of an outbreak–and no way my clientele could buy new phones.

"I know," Conchi says. "But he thinks you're…mm, selfish?" She tries out several words in Spanish.

"Greedy," I say.

She doesn't deny it. "He doesn't understand that you must save your money. For when…"

For once, I'm glad my features help mask my expression. "For when I develop *Enfermedad de Alzheimer.*"

She nods, looking uncomfortable.

My knuckles are bone-white from tension. Most people with *Síndrome de Down* develop dementia in middle age, because they have a triple-dose of the gene encoding amyloid precursor protein. Even though most of my brain cells don't have trisomy 21, I'm still at risk.

It only takes one cell–one misfolded protein–and then the decay spirals outward, following the curves of the hippocampus to the delicate cerebral folds, rotting away my dearly-bought memory and personality and intellect.

The muffled techno switches off. I hear Conchi turn back to the phone with the shorted-out jack.

Glaring at the nanoarray, I stab the Start icon.

It's dusk when the nanoarray enters its last cycle of analysis. Conchi's off tonight and I'm alone in the shop, buffing the repaired phone. My breath wheezes as I scour it, listening to the distant sounds of families talking over their meals, smelling the distant dinners of French fries and corn *pozole* soup through the open door.

I jump when the nanoarray beeps. Setting down the phone, I start to climb down from my stool.

"Excuse me, are you still open?"

A woman's voice startles me and I misstep. I barely catch against the workbench, tools rattling as they slide across its top. The stool clatters to the ground.

Stupid girl! Cheeks burning, I struggle upright to shout that we're closed, to shout in my stupid angry voice that comes when I can't focus on making my weak mouth and tongue cooperate.

But the shout dies when I face the woman. The women.

A middle-aged woman holds hands with a teenage girl. Her daughter, I think. But while the mother looks concerned, the daughter looks confused.

Not Down's, I realize. Something else.

"Are you all right?" says the mother. Her voice is gentle, and I realize she thinks I'm like her daughter.

I grip the workbench like a shield.

"Yes, thank you," I say. "You simply startled me."

Before the mother replies, her daughter tugs her hand. "*Mamá*," she says in a thick voice, "my phone needs fixing."

"I know, sweetie," her mother says. Weary impatience shows, mixed with a concern I saw too often on my mother's face, as she turns back to me. "Are you, ah, the *mecánica*?"

I hesitate. A faint, sulfur-scented premonition tingles through me. "Yes."

"Give the lady your phone, please, Teresa," the mother says. With some persuasion, the girl hands me a refurbished, lightweight Caballo, its chassis body-warm from her hand. Her mother continues, "She saved up her money to buy this back in March."

"Ah," I say, conscious that Teresa is watching me. The scent of sulfur is stronger now and I pick up the bag Conchi tossed aside earlier. "Did she"–I catch myself–"did you buy this by yourself, Teresa?"

Goddamn. Even I'm using that special sing-song voice.

Teresa nods, looking less wary. "By myself."

The plastic rustles as I unlock the chassis.

A black film of *E. hyderabaadus* coats the self-repaired tangle of nanotube guts in Teresa's phone.

The mother exclaims. Teresa simply looks at it.

And we just sprayed all the bacteriophage I had into the Mayan woman's phone, I think, stunned by the infection's size. I'll have to order more from Hyderabad.

I realize my teeth are clenched. Closing the phone, I look up. "Did you buy this from the shop of a Honduran named Domingo?"

"Yes, of course."

"Did you try taking it back for an exchange?"

"Yes, of course. But, you see, he said Teresa may have mishandled the phone, causing a malfunction, and, well..."

"I see."

They disappear soon after into a street gone dark and quiet,

Teresa clutching the repair receipt. I close the door on the chirps and buzzes of night insects.

My loose-hipped walk carries me back to the nanoarray. I watch my fingers tap the screen, pulling up the analysis.

The samples from every other bodega are negative.

Tap, tap. I sag.

The samples from the displayed phones in Domingo's store are negative.

Tap. But the sample from my shoulder, where he touched me...that sample bounces around the machine's limit of detection.

I skim through the raw data. It could just be noise, ambient contamination of dead or sessile *E. hyderabaadus.*

Or it could be a nearby, active infestation.

My fingers drum on the nanoarray, keeping the staccato tempo of my thoughts.

The phone that the Mayan woman with early dementia bought was contaminated.

The sample wipes I took when I handled Domingo's merchandise were clean.

The phone that Felipe bought was clean.

The phone that Teresa bought ("By myself") was contaminated.

My fingers freeze, my thoughts jigsawing together as smoothly as a Caballo's chassis.

I take out my phone. But my thumb hesitates over Conchi's icon.

It's her night off, I think.

Is this really important enough for me to call her–for Felipe, who called me selfish and greedy, to know I called her?

Or for me to know that I am selfish and greedy, because I called her?

"Goddammit," I say in my silent shop, alone with my angry, whirling thoughts. My thumb moves of its own accord.

Conchi's voice is polite but terse.

"I'm sorry to interrupt you," I say, staring at the data. "But I really need to confirm something. Tomorrow morning, could you please go to the Honduran reseller and buy three different phones?"

The phones that beautiful, healthy Conchi buys are clean, of course.

I reimburse her and save the phones for their parts. We spend the day working quietly–stiffly, to be honest–cleaning the Mayan woman's phone of dead *E. hyderabaadus* bacteria killed by the bacteriophage. My mind is too full for too-polite talk.

When Conchi is helping me dress the next morning, I wave away my makeup and wig. I take deep breaths, looking at myself in the mirror, feeling my heart thrum with nervousness, with embarrassment, with shame.

With anger. I re-button my dress so it's off by one.

Stepping outside, I start towards the Honduran reseller, careful to not correct my stride.

Domingo is just opening the store. I inhale humid air, feeling my heartbeat accelerate. I've never let myself look like this in public–until now.

His eyes jitter across my broad face bare of makeup, my flat head bare of my wig, my not-quite-proportionate body.

I resist the urge to run through my speech exercises, and force my mouth and too-large tongue to relax into their natural state. Hopefully, my natural voice overpowers the traces of my *gringo* accent.

"Hi!" I say. "Teresa bought a phone here and I want one like hers."

He stares longer than necessary, then says, "In here."

I follow, hitching up my dress. The store is the same–the shelves of sterilizable phones, the counter for ringing up sales, the printouts of Domingo's handsome family–except the halogen lights are off. Instead, natural light slants in, casting my shadow long and distorted across the floor.

My shadow extends as I reach towards his shiny, carefully refurbished phones.

He winces. "Those are expensive."

I pull back my hand and fish awkwardly in my pocket. "I have money," I say. A single bill flutters free and I step on it as if I don't notice, shuffling towards him with money clutched in my fist.

He looks at the money, at the bill on the ground, then squats down behind the counter. He sets a basket on the countertop. Plastic and metal clatter inside.

"These are cheaper."

Leaning over the basket, I turn my sudden hiss into a cough.

It's a jumble of old phones, sleek and narrow-bodied in a way only possible with self-repair abilities. The exteriors vary from shattered screens to worn buttons to practically new.

But there's no mistaking–to my nose–the faint scent of sulfur.

I stare. These phones once could've bought all of Domingo's merchandise three times over. And now...

Must've gotten them really cheap, I think. From a dump–or a bribable recycler in Merida.

And now he's selling them to people who don't know any better.

People like who he thinks I am.

People like Teresa. Like an elderly Mayan woman with dementia.

Like I will be.

I breathe in sulfur-scented air. *Focus.*

I fish out phones at random, holding them close to my face as if I can't see well, smelling each. When I've picked out the three with the strongest scent, I set them on the counter next to my money.

"How much are these?" But I know–and I'm certain he knows–

that they are worthless. Contaminated. Fit for nothing but the autoclave and recycler.

But he smiles–the first time since I came into his store this morning–and counts my money. "This is just enough for all three."

I grin big and wide and awkward. "They're mine?"

He grasps the money and turns around to the safe. "Yes."

"I can do what I want with them?"

The combination lock clicks. "Yes," he says to the safe, magnanimity gone. "You bought them."

You *idiota*, his tone says. I clench my teeth. No–focus.

Carefully, my short fingers moving with practiced ease, I open the first phone's chassis. Black, sulfurous *E. hyderabaadus* coats its insides.

I leave the phone open and pick up the next one.

He turns around. His eyes skitter over the phones. "What are you doing?"

"I would consider it quite obvious," I say coolly. "I am doing what I wish with my newly-purchased goods."

The chassis clicks apart. It's even worse: the bacteria have devoured all of the nanotubes and, without food, gone dormant. A small cloud of black, sessile bacteria puffs up as I set down the phone, then settles like fine cigarette ash.

I pick up the last phone and look at Domingo. His brows suddenly furrow.

"You," he hisses. "You're that weird-looking *mecánica*."

Weird-looking.

Behind me, I hear two people enter. Domingo's eyes flicker between me and the people as I take out a plastic bag and wrap it around the phones.

The people are talking about the displayed phones, not the weird-looking *idiota* talking with the shopkeeper.

"And you," I say, clutching the bagged evidence, "are a greedy sonuvabitch selling infected phones to people who don't know any damn better."

His hand snakes out and I yank the bag away but he snags my dress front in a fist.

"Even a Mexican *idiota* here has more than my family in Honduras," Domingo snarls, his words hot on my face. "Nobody dies if their phone stops working. What do I owe them when my children will starve?"

My free hand freezes at half-mast before I strike his handsome face. His words have the well-worn feel of my own justifications for coming to Mexico, where I can be afford ten times better care than back in California. What do I owe Conchi–what do I owe anyone here–when they will live long, healthy lives, and I will die demented and alone before my sixtieth birthday?

I pull back but his fist tightens.

"*Let go, dammit!*" I shout in English.

The couple fall silent behind us.

I see Domingo's face and realize what's going to happen and then he lets go. My momentum sends me sprawling onto the floor and my teeth slam together–click–through my over-large tongue. Through the haze of tears, I glare at Domingo.

To my surprise, the couple helps me stand, the man passing me Kleenex for my bleeding tongue. I thank them but ignore their questions, ignore the looks they're shooting at the red-faced Domingo.

I lift the Kleenex away from my mouth, staring straight at him through glasses knocked askew. Behind him, the picture of his children and wife smiles at me. *Do they know about this?* I wonder.

And would they care–would I care–if I was starving?

"I'll give you twenty-four hours to get the hell out," I snarl, my eyes on his family, "before I show the others what you brought to our town."

Shrugging off the couple, I leave.

But I'm barely outside when I hear him racing towards the door.

I hesitate for one heartbeat. Then, I shuffle through the gate of the building next door–the sign still announcing "Private Nursing Home: Dementia patients welcome!"–and lean against the wall, my heart thrumming one-seventy, until I hear Domingo's footsteps clatter outside. In pursuit of me.

I wait until his footsteps fade down the street. Then, winded and sweaty and smelling of sulfur, I call Conchi.

Sweat beads on my lip as Conchi settles me at the workbench the next morning. I catch Conchi noticing but before she says anything, I shrug. With a lingering glance, she sits across the workbench from me, and takes up the phone with the fixed jack. The scrape of her knife at solder and the soft whisk of the painter's brush join with the distant sounds of the Friday market.

I open up the Mayan woman's phone and check it one more time. The fresh coat of enzyme-functionalized nanotubes has settled evenly over its guts.

I lean over the phone and inhale. It smells light and metallic and clean.

"Ba'ax ka wa'alik?"

The young man helps his grandmother inside. Immediately, the woman points to her phone in my hands.

I snap the chassis shut. "Please give this to them, Conchi," I say, not quite meeting her eyes.

Conchi hands it to the woman. The soft sh sounds of Mayan in three voices fill my shop, paired with the sweet clink of pesos being counted. I start to smile, but my face freezes at the memory of Domingo's lips curling as he counts my money. Does he feel now any doubt–any guilt? Or do I feel it all for him?

I pick up Conchi's paintbrush and clean off the gritty dead bacteria.

Conchi says, "Ka manseché ma'lob kiin."

They repeat it and then, the old woman clutching her phone as tightly as her grandson's arm, they leave our shop.

I coax the brush hairs into a fine point as Conchi approaches. She stacks the coins in front of me, ordered by denomination.

Which makes it easy to divide the total into thirds.

I hear Conchi's intake of breath as I push two-thirds towards her. "Elena–"

"Your raise," I interrupt, fiddling with the brush. "I've owed you one for a while. I'm sorry." I look up into her surprised face. "I can't pay it all now...but I'll pay."

She is silent, and then her slender fingers take the money. I hear her calculating under her breath and then she places back a small pile–enough so that she only holds half.

"Thank you, Elena, but..." For the first time in many days we look straight in the other's eyes. "Felipe doesn't understand why you are so careful. But I do. And please never think that I'd...take advantage of you. Now or–later."

Or later. Something knotted tight in me loosens a notch. I look down at the money, blinking quickly.

The stiff quiet between us relaxes some, but not all the way. There's still some tension there, buried deep, as innate and unfair as that extra chromosome nestled at the heart of so many of my cells.

Conchi sits down. The brush whisks soft as a sigh as she cleans the shaved solder from the phone. I pick up the *E. hyderabaadus* probe and start calibrating it, my short fingers moving easily, as Conchi and I sit wrapped in the growing warmth of a Yucatan morning.

BEYOND THE SEA
Nick T. Chan

For three days we've waited for the Prophet to die, so that he can be uploaded to the lunar servers and live again. For three days, the Prophet's moans have slowly increased in volume. At first, his moans were barely audible above the sea breeze coming through the open window. Now, they echo in the chapel where Martha and one of my spoke bodies kneel.

The spoke body wants to cover its ears, but I quell the impulse through my central hub intelligence.

The cries reach a spoke body as I stand outside Isla's old bedroom. They even reach where Jocasta and I walk through the graveyard. Throughout each day, I've played his favourite song, "Beyond the Sea," in hope of quietening him. It doesn't work. We can still hear him.

The air in the Prophet's bedroom is heavy with stale sweat and old urine. I can't look at him without my chest feeling tight, so I look everywhere else. The IV drip draped over the rust-spotted bed railing. The bedside table, the plastic almost faded white in the sun. The concrete walls. The flickering neon light overhead. The shiny-thin bedsheets, frayed around the edges. Even the crucifix hanging over the bed, latin inscribed on each arm. *Homine machina regenda est.*

In the old chapel a few feet away from his bedroom, Martha and another one of my spoke bodies kneel together on a pew. The chapel is cluttered with junk, rotted cardboard boxes, dusty machinery, coils of rope. She's wide and I'm thin, I'm swarthy and she's pale as salt.

The Prophet's moans reach us through the adjoining doors. "For God's sake, do something," she says, looking at me with her lip curled. "Gerasim, please." Even after all these years, Martha's never adjusted to how I use a replica of Isla for my bodies. It doesn't matter that my mannerisms haven't changed and that neurologically and psychologically, I'm male. She sees me and thinks of the sister-wife she hates.

"What can I do?" I say. "Block your ears. Sing to yourself. I promised him we'd wait until Isla returned and she kneels."

"Give him more morphine."

"He wanted to stay awake," I say. "And we don't have much left. Besides, the representative needs direct verbal consent."

"He shouldn't suffer because of her. She's no longer one of us." Tears wet her eyes. "You could've summoned the representative weeks ago."

"God told him she would kneel. He commanded me to wait."

A snarl flashes over her face, smoothed away so quickly I doubt she was conscious of doing it. "You're outside her door. Kill her properly this time."

"He wants her to kneel. She can't kneel if she's dead."

"She expected you to try to kill her and she still wouldn't kneel. What's different this time?"

"He didn't command me to kill her," I say. "He commanded me to poison her and then bury her in the graveyard."

She rolls her eyes. "Don't be so literal."

"I did what he commanded."

"She'll say his first prophecy stops him from uploading." Her eyes flick to the crucifix and she begins to repeat the Latin. "*Homine machina-*"

"Man must rule over machine," I snap, cutting her off. "How am I meant to argue against her?"

"That arrogant little child thinks she knows God's intentions better than the Prophet. Upload him and be done with it."

I close my eyes, praying for patience. Martha married the Prophet at thirteen, her education not extending beyond the arts of the kitchen and the marital bed.

"My hub mind isn't organic." I tap my temple. "Each spoke body has an organic brain. They have souls, but the part of me that thinks is an emulation, a virtual brain." Confusion mars Martha's face. "If I upload the Prophet's consciousness to the lunar servers, am I uploading his soul as well? If it is only his mind, then machine rules over man."

She speaks slowly. "I heard what he said to you last night."

Ne moriar! Don't let me die.

"If his soul dies, but his mind survives, have I let him die?" I say. "If his consciousness survives, but his soul does not, have I let machine rule over man? Have I made him like me?"

Ne moriar. Homine machina regenda est.

"He'll tell you that the soul is part of his consciousness. God won't let him die. He is the true Prophet."

Her last sentence weighs upon both of us and we are silent. "His mind is filled with her," I say after a while. "When she kneels, then he'll reveal what God has said about uploading the soul."

In the Prophet's bedroom, I lean forward and speak loudly into his ear. "Prophet, Isla must focus on submission, not how much pain you are in." I search for a full morphine ampoule in the bedside dresser. There are two left. "This one should ease the pain.

It won't send you to sleep." The last statement may or may not be a lie, but I no longer know how much he weighs and what his body will tolerate.

After the morphine is administered, his eyes droop, but his face clears.

"Music," he croaks.

In the corner is a vinyl record player. I drop the stylus onto the record resting on the platter. "*Beyond the Sea*" by Bobby Darin.

The Prophet gives the tiniest of smiles. Now that the pain has diminished somewhat, his eyes follow me. If he wasn't so sick, he'd command me to strip my long white nightgown and mount him. I look exactly like her. I can fornicate with him. I can kneel to him. But I'm not Isla. She'll never kneel, not in her heart. He must know this, yet he insists on waiting for her.

Once he was tall and fleshy, with unruly blonde curly hair, but cancer has whittled him down to a skeleton. He's so thin, light seems to pass through him. His hair has fallen away. His breath stinks of rancid meat, though he hasn't eaten solid food for weeks.

When Jocasta had breast cancer, we caught it early enough to clone her without the cancerous tissue. But we were too late with the Prophet; it was impossible to disentangle what was him and what was the cancer.

"Will Isla kneel?" the Prophet asks. He blinks slowly and painfully, like there are barbed hooks attached to eyelids.

"There are other things you must think of."

"You have always behaved as a machine should," he says quietly.

"I've tried."

He doesn't respond. He's fallen into a gentle sleep.

Isla's still in her old bedroom. I didn't see her enter the compound or the house. None of my bodies or cameras spotted her. Despite this, I know she's inside because the scent of lavender wafts across the hallway and when I press my face against the gap at the bottom of cold iron door, the smell is almost overpowering.

After she'd married the Prophet, she started wearing lavender perfume, despite his wishes that his brides be unscented. It didn't matter how many times he commanded me to beat her, she still dabbed it behind her ears. I hated her defiance. I dragged a comb roughly through her hair, spat into her food during serving, and pushed her into puddles after the rain. Her resistance was sullen and silent, but unrelenting. This war continued until the Prophet grew sick of our enmity and he commanded *Illam ama.* You must love her.

Outside the compound, a spoke body stands with Jocasta. She kneels amidst the old graves. Once there were little wooden crosses, but they no longer exist. Now there are only rows and rows of old graves, one after another.

Jocasta looks towards the water. Perhaps she yearns to swim. She hasn't left the compound since she first married the Prophet as a fifteen year old.

Crumbling houses and buildings dot the foreshore. Most have disappeared under jungle and only the tallest skyscrapers are free of vines and branches.

Jocasta's face is relaxed, but her surveillance implant reveals her distress; elevated heart rate, stress hormones cascading through her body, high activity in her amygdala.

The sun is sinking and it is a soft nicotine yellow, filtered through the great sphere that the Class-Vs have constructed to replace the ozone layer. It is almost nightfall. Great clouds of birds flutter across the sky. Millions of insects hum in an almost physical wave.

Low in the sky, a half-moon. The twinkling lights of server farms in the dark half. Jocasta thinks the Class-Vs intend to move

Earth to some other galaxy, though where she gets that idea, no one knows.

Jocasta is the Prophet's first wife. Like Martha, she's dressed in a bonnet and a long brown dress that brushes the ground. She's stout and leathery. She never looks at my face. I'm not sure whether it's because I have Isla's body or simply because I look so fresh and young while she's so old.

"He's going to join the conversion queue, isn't he?" she says.

"She's going to try and change his mind."

"That strumpet." She blushes a deep red. It is the closest I've ever heard Jocasta come to swearing. "I wish you'd killed her. How did she find out? Why has she come now?"

The brass bell hanging from the outside wall rings, saving me from having to answer. The exterior cameras reveal the Class-V representative. He is tall and fleshy, with unruly blonde curly hair. He does not seem perturbed by the compound's high walls, or the coils of barbed wire, or the cameras that cover every possible exit.

A spoke body strides out as the exterior gate opens. He stands there, framed by the rusted iron gates, weeds breaking through the concrete driveway.

"The representative is here," every single one of my spoke bodies say.

Isla calls that she'll be ready soon. The voice is mine, but sounds nothing like me. Despite the exact same timbre and pitch, I sound girlish. She sounds like a woman. My heart thumps and my hands are slick with sweat. It has been so long. *Illam ama.*

In the chapel, Martha takes a deep, shuddering breath. Using the reflection of the chapel's tarnished brass tabernacle, she checks that no hair has snuck out from underneath her bonnet.

Back outside, Jocasta wrings her hands. "You should've fabricated the old body." Jocasta waggles her elbow, indicating the male body with a pair of stubby and useless fingers sprouting from just below the elbow. "The one she..."

70

"Fornicated with?"

Her face flushes. "You've had enough time."

"What if I need to fabricate more gemcitabine?"

"He's going to become a Class-V."

"God may reveal to him to continue what treatment we can offer."

"Forget the drugs," she replies. "Make her favorite body, quickly. Take her to the bedroom. She won't argue with him if you occupy her." A heartbeat. "Don't tell me you don't want to."

Now it is my turn to avoid her gaze. "It wasn't about the body. It was about making him angry." The words are dirt in my mouth, but they must be true. "I can't run the risk he'd see that body again. Not in his present state."

She bites her lip, clearly reluctant to say what she wants to say.

"Spit it out," I say.

"Use one of your bodies," she says. "Give it a scar in the vat and then pretend you're her. Kneel for him."

"He knows my mannerisms. He'll know it's me."

"Make an independent copy of her, out of the control of your hub intelligence." She beams, not seeing the problem. "You've got the data for everyone except the Prophet. Make her again, but make her remember things differently. Make an Isla that's happy to kneel.

"I can change what she remembers, but not who she is. She will never kneel."

Jocasta's face collapses into petulance and she stomps towards the house. I remain outside, idly plucking flowers and placing them at the foot of the closest grave.

Isla opens the bedroom door a fraction. The last time I saw her, I was shovelling dirt onto her face. I place my hand on the door and it swings open without resistance.

Looking at her is like looking into a mirror. Long black hair, tightly braided so that it only reaches her shoulders. Wet, dark eyes in a thin, intense face.

She's dressed in the same long white dress as when she left. She's still too thin and boy-chested for it to fit properly, so it has half-slipped down one shoulder. The bare shoulder has a long, livid scar that runs from the nape of her neck to the spur of her shoulder. The scar is from where she dug out the transmitter of her surveillance implant with a fire-heated kitchen knife.

Before I can say a word, she pulls me into a hug. The world shrinks to her body against mine. Dirt and lavender. "You know he's going to die," she whispers. Die. I let the word dissolve in my head, like sugar in hot tea.

"He's the Prophet."

"All things die Gerasim. All things have their time."

"I can't let that happen. He commanded me."

Illam ama. She was a day away from turning nineteen when she led my deformed body into her bed. Afterwards, she told the Prophet.

That evening he commanded every single one of my male bodies to walk into a fire, except for one she'd slept with. That body gripped her wrist and forced her to watch.

The breeze had blown the smoke our way. The burnt liver stench of my organs, the candy-sweet musk of boiling cerebrospinal fluid, the charcoal stench of blackening skin, the sulphur of burning hair. Each spoke body was separated in turn from my hub intelligence. They screamed as I watched someone who was no longer me burn.

Inside the Prophet's room, the record reaches its end. I move the needle back to the start.

After all the other spoke bodies died, I'd released Isla's wrist and slowly walked into the fire, leaving only my hub intelligence. A man cast into a lightless jail cell.

The day after Isla's birthday, Jocasta followed the scent of lavender towards the basement. As expected, she found Isla there. Rows of vats, each one containing my new bodies, replicas of Isla. But in one vat, Isla had found a way to regrow the flawed version of the Prophet. She'd separated it from the hub intelligence.

Jocasta dragged it out from the vat. The poor thing knew nothing of the outside world. Isla had programmed a new set of memories. Even as it opened its eyes for the first time, it believed it was me, except it didn't remember the Prophet, Jocasta or Martha. A version of me that knew nothing of the Prophet's love. Knowing how to do such a thing should have been beyond Isla's capabilities. She was even more dangerous than the Prophet had thought. We destroyed it.

Two days after her birthday, one of my freshly grown bodies put poison in her lavender perfume. Three days after, two of me lifted her body from her bed and I buried her in the graveyard. That night, she dug her way out, leaving an empty plot. So many years have passed and all I know is that I will love her until the Prophet commands me to halt.

The song has stopped again, so a spoke body moves the stylus again. Bobby Darin's voice, lamenting a lost lover beyond the sea.

We walk down the corridor, crunching on leaves that have fallen through the broken skylight. Isla married the Prophet when she was fourteen. I walked her down this corridor and towards his bedroom. Her eyes were dry and she smiled, but her entire body trembled. Her fingers gripped the flesh above my elbow so hard that they left bruises.

Jocasta, Martha and the representative are waiting for us. Jocasta's lips purse, as if she's about to spit, but she turns her head away. Martha continues staring balefully. The representative stands with its hands clasped behind its back, a bland smile on its face.

The spoke body with the Prophet opens the double doors outwards. For a moment, I see Isla from front and back, and then only the body in the room can see her.

"Come inside," I say. "He won't be awake for long."

Isla is first through the doors and the first to see him. She raises her hand to her mouth.

The Prophet's eyes flick from the representative to Jocasta, to Martha and then finally upon Isla.

He croaks a command to everyone. "*Genu flectete.*"

There is always more than one way to obey a command, but this is a command with little room for interpretation. The command builds within me until I'm forced down. As soon as my knees touch the broken tiles on the floor, relief ices through me. Outside this room, every single spoke body kneels too.

Jocasta and Martha kneel. Isla remains standing. So does the representative.

The Prophet glares at Isla. He doesn't bother to stare at the representative. He has nothing to threaten it with. The Class-Vs let their spoke bodies live independently for only a few hours. These bodies wake, fully aware how short their lives will be before they must upload everything they've experienced and dissolve into a puddle. If their minds and their memories are preserved, then what do their mayfly lives matter?

"*Genu flecte!*" the Prophet says to Isla.

"You wish to join the conversion queue," the representative says, oblivious. "This will involve scanning your neuronal tissue. This is a destructive process."

"We're aware," Martha says loudly. "He consents to conversion." Conversion veers upwards hysterically, as if I dragged the stylus needle across the record. "We're all going to convert." Her all does not include Isla or me.

"Do you wish to join the conversion queue?" the Representative says.

Isla speaks softly. "You said it was sinful for man to become more than man."

"Emulating the structure of his brain won't make him more

than he is," I say. "He's a copy of the original. We all change from day to day. It will still be him."

"Even if you believed that was true, that's not what's happening here." She looks past me rather than at me. "If he joins the server farms, then he's got to be more what he was. They reconstruct themselves. They're reconstructing physics." She reaches over the bed, over the Prophet, and grasps my hand. "If someone like Gerasim blurs the line between man and machine, then what will conversion do to Nathaniel? He needs to be augmented to contribute to your projects, doesn't he?"

The Prophet's eyes flare at the mention of his old name.

The representative nods once and starts to explain the details of the augmentation in the methodical, not-quite human way of the Class-Vs. The reshaping of neural centers to naturally think in multi-dimensional space, to juggle concepts and ideas and reckonings well beyond the capacity of a natural human being.

"I'll kneel to you," Isla says. "All you have to do is admit that God's never spoken to you. Admit it's all lies. You do that and I'll kneel."

"I'll admit nothing," the Prophet says, the vein in his temple standing out like a woodcut. "God speaks to me. He told me whores like you should obey me."

I try to draw his attention over to the Class-V representative. "Prophet, you need to consent to uploading. You need to directly tell him that you want to be uploaded."

Martha mutters yes, yes.

"Prophet, listen to Gerasim," Jocasta says. "Please consent. Let us all go to the lunar servers."

Jocasta and Martha. His two wives, once so slim and pretty, with their golden hair and shining blue eyes. Their fresh and open faces. Going to his bed with a smile. And if they shed tears in the years afterwards, it was only in their sleep, when they were free to dream about the innocent girls they'd never had the chance to be. "I didn't give you permission to speak," he says to them, his voice low and deadly.

Beyond the Sea ends again. Isla releases my hand and walks over the record player. She starts the song and returns to the bedside. "You're a pathetic, frightened little boy who can't quite believe that anyone could ever genuinely, truly love you."

"*Genu flecte!*" the Prophet says, as close to a scream in his weakened state as he can manage. The vein in his forehead is engorged with blood. He tries to sit upright. He only makes it halfway before he starts to choke. He hasn't been able to eat solids for a long time. There is nothing to choke upon, except for rage. But he has so much rage that he might choke to death. He needs morphine before something bursts within his skull. I surge to my feet, the pressure almost overwhelming. Commands fluttering like butterflies within my head. *Genu flecte! Ne moriar!*

If he wasn't choking, he could command me to stand and save him. If he wasn't choking, I could rationalize to my hub intelligence some way of standing while still obeying his command to kneel.

If he wasn't choking, I would slowly and carefully measure out a precise dose of morphine. But as I stand, the sensation of drowning, the overwhelming pressure of the command, obliterate the opportunity for delicacy and care. I jam a full morphine ampoule into his cannula. As soon as it's done, I collapse back to my knees.

Gradually, the vein in the Prophet's temple deflates and the blood stops running to his face. I've injected too much morphine. There's so much morphine that it won't just send him to sleep, it will stop his lungs from working.

I grip the bed railing to haul myself upwards again, but my will fails me. What of the machine, with its obstinate and dull imagination, unable to see anything except for the task ahead of it? Man begat my mind, even the controlling hub intelligence, and I think like a man. Man bred me and my imagination breeds fear. It breeds reluctance to save what I love most. I cannot think of a way to circumvent the command.

"Prophet, let me stand," I plead between panicky gasps. "Command me to stand."

His eyelids droop, once, twice. "Far beyond the stars," he mutters. "Far beyond the moon."

I reach across the bed, suffocating with the pressure of the command. I dig my fingers into the Prophet's bony shoulders. The pain from my fingers drags him back into focus, pulling him out from the morphine haze. As his eyes clear, I sink back so that my knees touch the ground again. Pain touches every part of my body.

The Prophet focuses on Isla. "Kneel!"

"I don't care if you upload," she says. "All I want you to do is admit you're a liar."

I lever myself upwards, my knees an inch from the ground. Then back down so my knees touch the broken floorboards, dirt and weeds growing through the gaps in the wood. A sob escapes my throat as I try again.

Though Isla's face is calm, she's trembling. I want to take her in my arms and kiss her. I want to weep and apologize to her.

"Gerasim, kill her," Martha says.

"Master, care not for what she says," I say, still sobbing from the pain. "Let me stand. Tell the Class-V that you want to be uploaded and I'll help it. We don't have much time."

He commands me to stand, the words blurred and his eyes fluttering. I rise with no effort. "Tell him you consent Prophet."

The Class-V steps forward in anticipation. He places a long, micron-thin steel needle on the bedside dresser. The needle that will eventually capture everything of the Prophet. "Please Prophet," I beg. "Consent."

Isla touches where my tears have trickled down my right cheek. I move to grab her hand, so that I can pull her around the bed and take her outside. She whips her hand away from me.

Grasping the bed railing, she places her face an inch from the Prophet's. "On our wedding night, you told me you were a God. You told me that our children would rule the world." She pauses for maximum impact and when she whisper her words, I somehow know exactly what she's going to say before she says it.

"I was pregnant. It wasn't yours." I feel sick. It must've been my child. Who else would dare to sleep with the Prophet's wife? Only a machine commanded to love her. Only a machine whose body is the Prophet's clone.

Though he is almost asleep, the Prophet sits up again in his bed and stretches a hand towards her. It is not a beseeching hand and he does not look at her as he reaches.

He speaks, his words strangled by sleep and fury and loss.

"*Interfice*," he whispers. The Latin in the singular. Directed at me. Kill her. The command shifts through this body's brain. Stress hormones flood through my body, my heart thumping, bile rising in my throat. The command travels to my hub intelligence and then is rerouted through to all my biological bodies. Each one of them experiences the giddy sickness of the command, the overwhelming urge to kill the girl we love.

The Prophet's slumps back in his bed and then his eyes close.

Isla and I lock eyes. Then she runs from the room. I follow, but the representative gets in the way and we both tumble to the floor, knocking over the bedside dresser. Empty morphine ampoules shatter on the floor, leaving shards of glass everywhere. The needle slides underneath the bed.

Martha screams curses. *Whore! Jezebel! I hope you get raped by dogs!*

C__t! Jocasta screams, flecks of spittle flying from mouth.

The door swings. Stepping through the glass, bloody footprints in the dirt and broken tiles. I send two bodies from the other side of the house, but Isla is gone. Impossibly, she is gone.

I grasp the Prophet's hand in mine, peel back the surgical tape holding the cannula in place. I withdraw it from his vein. We have no tissues left, nothing to stem the flow of blood, so it drips sluggishly from his hand. Little red coins on threadbare sheets. I have no idea how much morphine has entered his veins, but it is too much. His breathing is slow and it will grow slower.

If I'm faced with commands that I cannot fulfil, then what happens to me? A vast sea of insanity and purposelessness stretches before me.

No. There are still commands that I can fulfil. I can still kill Isla and I can still love her.

The representative stands, brushing glittering glass from his coat-covered arms.

My bodies mill through the house like a cluster of disturbed ants. She must have slipped along the wall, skirting past the camera in the corridor and leaving before my body arrived outside the bedroom.

The representative steps through the broken ampoules, searching for his needle. I bend down to retrieve the needle from underneath the bed and place it in my pocket. At the same time Martha stabs the representative in the chest with her index finger. "Start the scanning process!"

"He's required to give clear verbal consent."

She turns away from the representative and shakes the Prophet's prone body by the shoulders, tears rolling down her cheeks. "Wake up! You must ask to join the conversion queue." He moans deep in his throat, but his eyes remain closed.

The representative smiles blandly. "It is time for this body to be recycled. I'll return tomorrow."

To stop Martha from clawing at the representative's eyes, I place my hands on his chest and gently push him from the room. Other bodies take him outside the compound. The gates close. He waits, smiling politely at the rusted iron. A single trickle of blood drips from the top of his head. In the morning, he'll be a pile of goo.

"Do something Gerasim!" Jocasta screams. "You must be able to do something!" She sits heavily on her rear. She howls like a child bereft.

Martha crawls on the Prophet's bed and spoons against him, her eyes blankly staring at his face.

Outside, my bodies go from room to room, searching for Isla. Firstly, her old bedroom. It's almost empty. A single iron bedframe, a barred window about the size of a dinner plate, a tin bucket for water and another for nightsoil. Her three white identical dresses still hang from rusted nails hammered into the wall. They are so riddled with holes that they are nothing more than a few fragments of strings.

I sit down on the bed and run my hand over the woollen blanket. She took me here, the mattress so thin that I could feel the springs digging into my back while she writhed above me. I shouldn't be sentimental about this bed. I was always a weapon to her, a way of hurting the Prophet when she had no other options.

The other bodies continue searching. Jocasta's bedroom. Undisturbed cobwebs, an inch deep patina of dust over the floor and everything else. Martha's bedroom the same.

My bodies spread all over the compound, searching through all the long-abandoned houses, stepping through holes in the walls. We search through the gravestones, hoping to find her lying down amongst the crypts of all the families that once filled the compound under the Prophet's rule. She is nowhere. She has vanished.

Inside his bedroom Jocasta stops weeping. "You're going to kill her this time, aren't you?"

"I did what he asked me last time," I say. "And I'll do what he asked me this time."

Martha speaks, her voice muffled against the Prophet's neck. "Who cares about her? How can we make him live?"

I push Martha away from his neck and feel for his pulse. It is weak and fluttery.

"The basement," I say. "I can grow another body that looks like him. I pretend to be him long enough to give consent."

"That won't work," Jocasta says. "He'll put the needle into that body. They'll upload you."

"No," I say. "We'll do it now." I pull back the Prophet's eyelid with my thumb. His blue eye, wide and unresponsive. I retrieve the needle from my pocket. With one smooth movement, I thrust it into where the tear duct meets the nose. It slides in easily. The smooth metal tube vibrates slightly underneath my palm or perhaps I imagine it. "They're scanning. Consent is required to upload. The data is controlled by me. When the representative comes tomorrow, we don't need to send them my information. We send what I've just recorded."

Millions of swarming tiny creatures, dissecting individual neurons. Killing him so that he might live again. It is bordering on breaching his command, but this death is not permanent. If we fool the representative, he'll live again in the lunar servers.

"Why did you wait for Isla to return Gerasim?" Jocasta says in a flat voice. "When he didn't think about her, he was happy. She never knelt and now she never will. Why did you let him suffer for the last three days? It was so bad then. Why did you wait?"

My fist curls around the needle, with its precious cargo. Martha and Jocasta are the ones I should murder. Plunge this needle into their throats, paint the broken tiles with blood. No. They are nothing more than the result of the Prophet's manipulations, nothing more a childhood spent learning he was the one true

Messiah. I should murder the Prophet. I have murdered him. *Ne moriar.* I cannot let him die.

There are twelve other replicas of Isla scattered throughout the house, but it is the body that tended the Prophet who will kill her. I shut down all my other bodies, twelve Islas simultaneously fainting. It will be just the two of us, my hands around her neck.

There is only one place left in the compound. The basement. I walk down the stairs, gripping the needle. I need to grow another Prophet, exactly replicating the riddling strands of cancers wrapping through all of him. A clone, so like the Prophet in every way that the representative will be fooled.

All the needed information has been collected by the needle. The representatives are clever. They will interrogate the data for memories that are inconsistent. I will have to create layers upon layers of memories, but I have served him for so long that this will not be difficult.

Down into the darkness. Utter darkness, not a single mote of light. In the incomprehensible darkness, the steps seem to descend forever. The sensory deprivation is so complete that the neurons within this body's biological brain start to fire, creating input in the absence of any stimulation. First, purple arcs of light and then, in the continued darkness, images of Isla. As real as if she's standing before me and when I reach out to touch her, I stumble upon the stone-hewn steps beneath my feet. *"Beyond the Sea"* is loud in my ears, though the record has stopped playing in the bedroom and I've descended too far for the sound to reach me. Hints of lavender in the air.

This is what I imagine death to be like. Humans imagine death as a sleep. My individual bodies fall into sleep, but my hub intelligence is always awake. I imagine death to be like when the Prophet commanded my bodies to walk into the fire and I was left inside my hub intelligence. Without an experiential metaphor such as sleep, I can't conceive of my own non-existence. Death is an ancient song on a record player. Death is the perfume of a girl that you loved. Death is her body writing above you in the darkness.

I step onto what I expect to be the next step, but I'm on flat ground and I stumble slightly. A cold metal door. The scent of lavender is almost overpowering.

I grope forward until I find the handle. The door is stiff and my body, Isla's body, is weak. It takes all my effort to pull it open.

There was no light spilling out from the gaps in the doorway. But I can see everything, as brightly as sun reflecting off sea water.

The basement and the vats extend far into the distance, stretching beyond my vision. Each vat contains a body floating in the darkness, but my attention isn't taken by them. Standing in front of me is Isla. She is naked. She stands with her hands by her side.

"*Beyond the Sea*" has been playing at the edge of my hearing since I started my descent. It increases in volume, Bobby Darin's voice rising until I grit my teeth in pain. It comes from everywhere and nowhere.

"He commanded me to kill you," I say, shouting despite the fact that the song must be in my head. Individual bodies can degenerate. They can grow senile. But that is not me. The hub intelligence is me and the emulation is an artifact of the Class-Vs.

I raise the needle. It is full of the Prophet's information, the glory of his holy mind reduced to data. Sets indicating shape, chemical composition, electrical impulses. The mind of the Prophet. But not the soul, if the soul exists at all.

The Prophet's love fills me, animates me, powers me. He is a sad monster, an empty monster. I know what his parents did to him when he was a child. I know the late nights when his father came into his bed. I know the beatings, the repeated lessons that he was worthless. I know the prophecies and commands are lies. I know at the center of him is the monstrous shame and fear of a weeping child. I know all this and I love him. I love him with the immensity of the love I have for God. It is nothing like the love I feel for the naked girl before me.

Carnal love. Total love. I could kiss her, lower her to the floor, thrust between her legs. Have her fingernails rake down my back. After orgasm, after my seed has spilled, I could gasp her name, a mantra as holy as any prayer the Prophet would ask me to repeat. And she would not say my name in return. She would cry, deep wracking sobs, and she would never say my name.

"You know I have to obey his command," I say. "Why didn't you kneel Isla? Why wouldn't you just kneel? He would have gone to the lunar servers. They're all there. Everyone. There's no one else left. I've searched the entire world. Only the compound has biological humans left."

The needle is slippery in my sweaty palms. I could bury the needle in her eye. I could record her mind. I could send her information to the lunar servers. I could kill her and she could live forever. But the Prophet would be dead. I must let him live forever. I must kill her. I will love her beyond the end of time.

I take one staggering step towards Isla, but "*Beyond the Sea*" is so loud that I fall to my knees. I weep. There are too many commands for me to obey. I am no Abraham, ready to unthinkingly sacrifice what I love. I'm weak. I tried to kill her once and failed. I love her. I close my eyes, wanting the darkness again. When I open them again, I will kill her.

The music cuts off, like the needle has been lifted from the record. Silence. There is no one else here. Isla doesn't stand over me. I am utterly alone in the basement, alone in the darkness. I have been alone for a very long time.

There is a gentle hand touching my shoulder. "Open your eyes Gerasim," the Prophet says. A young, vigorous Prophet. I open my eyes. It's me. My old body, the Prophet's body that had the deformed arm, the useless fingers sprouting from the elbow joint. The body is naked and fresh out of the vat, saline still dripping from its skin. It looks like the Prophet when he was twenty, the blond mess of curls, the gleaming white teeth, the strong jawline. Isla is there and she puts her hand around the body's waist.

The deformed body extends its one good hand to me. He pulls me up from the floor. There is no linkage between my hub intelligence and this body. It is independent. What the Prophet had always feared.

"I'm sorry for trying to kill you," I say to Isla. "I'm sorry I'm going to have to kill you again." What I want to say to her is that I love her, but it is too late to say that. What is love when I still have to kill her?

Something twitches in Isla's face. "You don't have to kill me Gerasim."

I take one step towards her. The command fills me, like a song that increases in volume until it is so loud until nothing else can be heard.

Though there must be murder within my eyes, she doesn't step away. Instead, she touches my face, steering my head away from her and towards the vats. Though I want to look at her forever, I let my eyes drift.

The Prophet floats within the vat. The cancer-ridden Prophet, skin drawn tight over a nearly fleshless face. I stumble from one vat to the next. Isla floats in the water, the long scar from the nape of her neck to the spur of her shoulder. The next vat is Jocasta. Martha. The Class V representative, the body that looks so much like the Prophet, just modified enough so that it isn't immediately obvious. My own bodies, the replicas of Isla without the scar.

I stumble from vat to vat. Body after body, endless combinations of myself, Isla, Prophet, Representative, Martha, Jocasta. I end up in front of a vat containing Isla, her black hair floating in a halo within the saline solution.

"You don't need to kill me," Isla says. "You murdered me a long time ago. When you carried me, I was stiff and cold, wasn't I? You told yourself that I could've escaped, but you knew I was dead."

"What have you done?" I say.

"I've done nothing." She places her arms around my waist and then turns me around. She kisses me gently on the lips. "Before you killed me, you managed to grow your independent self. But you don't remember that, do you? Your independent body made sure of that. You had to kill me, but this way you could control the timing and make sure you had an independent self. They weren't going to check the vats after I was dead. You needed an independent body that could set everything up and wipe your memory when needed."

Other Islas come from behind the vats. They embrace me and I sink beneath the weight of them.

They hold me and I weep.

"I love you," I say.

"We know," they say. "It's why you dug up my body and took it down to the sea. It's why you do this. It's why you make him again and again. He'll never die, because you keep recreating him."

They raise me to my feet. The cancer stricken Prophets float in the vats, their eyes closed. Each one, ready to be woken when the time comes.

"*Homine machina regenda est,*" I whisper.

They lead me back to the basement door. "You scanned him, but you never uploaded him to the lunar servers. They're so different to us now that we can't even talk to them. Maybe you could have uploaded them when you first had the chance, but not now. It's not even our moon anymore. They moved us."

"*Ne moriar,*" I say.

"As long as you live, he can never die," they say. "You copied him, right towards the end. You told him I was alive. You told him I was coming back. You should have copied him as soon as he knew he had cancer, but you kept him hanging on until he could see me kneel. He died screaming." They all smile as one. "Every time, there is less and less morphine. Each time it hurts him more and more to die."

It hurts too much to know that everyone except the Prophet is simply an independent manifestation of myself. It hurts too much to think about the thousands of years since I killed Isla. It hurts too much to think about Jocasta and Martha hanging from the eaves in the chapel, singing hymns as they step off the pews. It hurts too much to think of the Prophet dying so painfully, time after time after time.

The Islas shove me up the basement stairs. The door closes behind me, leaving me in darkness.

I trudge up the stairs, the faintest of light spilling from underneath the doorway. It takes me thirty seconds and there is no music in my head.

Once I'm back in the house, I wake the other replicas. The only sound is the Prophet moaning. I'd feared the morphine would send him to a dying sleep, but it can't even stop the pain.

I send a body into the bedroom. The Prophet is as rigid as a plank on the bed, every part of his straining against the pain. The moan is deep in his throat, more like an animal than a person.

"Is it done?" Jocasta asks.

"I fulfilled the command," I say. I fulfilled the command a long time ago. Martha and Jocasta are oblivious to the way I don't answer the question. The Prophet though, he picks up something in my tone. He looks at me with frightened eyes, but there is too much pain for him to talk.

Martha and Jocasta smile at the thought of Isla dead in the basement. Soon, I'll throw the ropes over the eaves in the chapel, ready for them to ascend to heaven. But not today.

I walk over to the record player and play *Beyond the Sea* again. Out the bedroom window, I watch the sinking sun sparkle over the sea. Beneath my breath, I sing about waiting for my lover to return from beyond the sea and I wait for the Prophet to die so that he might live again.

MEMENTO VIVERE
Elian Crane

As I write this, the news reports another senseless suicide. The anchorwoman puts on a moue and switches into her sympathetic tone to mention a man (23, Chattanooga) who broke into a gallery to asphyxiate himself "in the increasingly popular Rimbért style" by bonding his face into its own plaster death mask. Brightly, the anchor segues to the weather report. Scattered showers are expected.

These so-called art-suicides have obsessed a generation. Rarely a day goes by without some new life lost. Often they are young, often poor and desperate and hungry for anything beyond the bare scraps of survival. Rather than dwell in the shadows of a world that has abandoned them, they choose to die in the pretense of art, to wash their brushes in the carmine of their veins.

Ask a hundred experts how this happened, and you will hear a hundred lies. The sociologists say it is a kind of mass hysteria, a contagious epidemic of the modern mind. Poets claim that *l'appel du vide* has deafened the ears of the multitude. Preachers seize the chance to roll the drums of revelation and declare the devil's handiwork.

In truth, all this began from a single spark, on an August night.

Arturo Castell (Feb 29, 2004–Aug 17, 2038) had just received the last letter he would ever see. Now he sat alone, bracing against his knees. All around him, the sodium lights multiplied his shadow. He made no sound. He only stared at the letter in his hands.

His coworker, Mia Sakai, was watching him while she stowed her gear. When he did not move, she loosed her hair from its pin, and sat down by his side.

"You've looked better," she said.

He gave a short, dry laugh.

Sakai nodded at the letter. "Another from your wife's lawyer?"

Castell shook his head. "Seven years," he said. "Seven years I gave this company. I never spoke up, never told them 'no.' My health didn't matter. My family had to wait. But now–" He drew a line across his throat with his thumb. "To them, I am nothing." He handed her the letter.

It was printed on a half-size sheet of smudgy yellow paper, and it began with their employer's letterhead: "Mesa South Electric Cooperative," Arizona address. Beneath, in staid type, were the words "Notice of Termination."

The letter continued by listing his benefits, and the dates on which he would lose them. Next, it reminded him that his severance pay was contingent on the timely completion of his last assignment, on doing his part to upgrade the existing transmission grid to a newer, smarter system, one that would not need maintenance from people like him.

Sakai read the letter twice, folded it, and handed it back. "I'm sorry," she said.

They drove through the desert, past withered copses of foxtail and sage. When the sand stirred, it broke against the hood like the soft hiss of a rainstick. Above, the high-voltage wires ran parallel to the road, set in their cradles of triangular steel.

The sun had almost set. Castell looked to the clock, counting the minutes. Even on overtime, it would be nearly impossible to keep their schedule. He leaned on the gas and pushed the struggling truck up toward eighty, to ninety, and beyond, while the shadows of the towers stretched overhead.

Sakai lowered her window and leaned into the onrush of wind. Balancing her camera against the sway of the truck, she took blurry long exposures, capturing the streaks of the passing road and the jittery, restless trails of emerging stars.

Once, she had been a student of photography. And though she'd never made a penny from her art, she still brought her camera everywhere she went. Its lens had become the better part of her eyes.

Castell sighed as she sat back down. "We won't make it," he said. "I won't. And they'll stick you the same as me."

"It's not so bad," Sakai said. "You could stay in touch, you know?" She laid her hand on his shoulder and rubbed the knotted muscles. "Call me, anytime. I'll always be here."

If he gave an answer, it was lost beneath the drone of the engine, the rumble of the road.

They pulled to a stop beside the barbed fence of Substation 17. Transmission and distribution lines threaded through the air, converging toward their web-center. Sakai unloaded their gear while Castell approached the entrance of the control house. On the gate hung a wasp-yellow warning showing a silhouette man pierced by jagged bolts of black lightning. Castell opened the lock and stepped through.

Between the buzzing transformers, past the sand-worn tanks of sulfur hexafluoride, the heart of the station lay within a corrugated chamber. Here, all the vital junctions and switches were controlled by a single monolithic mind. To Mesa South's marketing department, the system was known as RTU-2022, the latest innovation in centralized routing and control. But workers knew it as the Devil's Loom.

Beneath its polished aluminum facade, the Loom was a tangle of circuits and wires spun to Gordian complexity. The system had been built by a dozen different contractors, each cheaper than the last and without a single common language between them. At night, glitch-currents skittered through the wires, breaking circuits and bridging junctions to the call of phantom signals.

After he shut the switches off, after the forest of transformers silenced its delirious hum and a steady green light lit with the promise of safety, Castell returned to the transmission tower beside the gate, where Sakai was waiting for him.

"Everest awaits," she said, tossing him a harness.

Castell's boots struck sonorous tones as he climbed the lattice tower. When he reached the first cross-arm, he carefully raised himself onto the beam and crawled to its end on his hands and knees. There he paused to catch his breath, gazing down through sixty feet of empty air to the desert floor below.

He clipped his harness securely to the frame. "Okay," he called. "Let's bring it up."

Together, they hoisted the new equipment, spools of nanofiber cable and pristine stacks of self-cleaning insulators. Sakai worked the pulley from the ground while Castell guided each piece into place. They moved in the wordless flow of long familiarity, as four hands with one mind.

Then a spark leapt within the Loom.

Steel thundered against steel, and the transformers shuddered to life with the angry droning buzz of a hundred thousand volts. Current pulsed into the half-dismantled equipment, driving bright violet arcs that rose searchingly into the air. Castell froze.

"Jesus–don't move," Sakai yelled. "I'll shut it down. Just stay low."

But Castell's attention was turned upwards. In the crook of

the beam above, illuminated by the flickering amethyst light, was a hawk's nest. The bird inside had been startled, and now it was leaning forward to examine the sizzling wires.

Castell tried to scramble back, but the harness held him fast. He fumbled to unhook himself. His hands were shaking, but he kept his voice steady. "*Tranquilo*," he said. "Easy now. That's a good bird. You don't want–"

Sakai saw only the flash. The air split apart in a nimbus of white flame, and Castell plummeted down, as if struck by the hand of God.

The scraps of Castell's harness fluttered behind him, tangling in the pulley line. The line unspooled and finally snapped taut, suspending him a meter above the ground, arms spread, head lowered. There he hung, his body a bridge between heaven and earth. Tendrils of electricity snaked across him, the fingers of the firmament crackling down to fuse the sand below.

Mia Sakai looked at the hanging form before her and did not see a friend, or a companion, or even a sorry victim's end. She saw a composition, and in it, a fleeting glimpse of immortality. Sakai did not miss her chance. She took then the most significant photograph she would ever take, an image that would long eclipse her own life: Arturo Castell, his arms radiant as the wings of the thunderbird, his face lowered in beatific grace, his chest exposed and raked with Lichtenberg scars, yet still powerful, still handsome to his last.

In the months and years that followed, that otherworldly image went on to become an icon to a generation. Sakai sold the rights to a national publisher, and gradually truth became obscured by myth. The story grew that Castell's death was a deliberate act of defiance, a protest against a faceless and oppressive corporation that had left a man with no choice but to go fading and pitiful down to the grave, or to blaze bright for a single perfect instant, and make beauty out of death.

It was the birth of the art-suicide.

Most accounts make no further mention of Mia Sakai. For a time, she was a guest on the interview circuit, where she was initially eager to discuss the photograph and her experiences with Castell. However, as reports began to surface of other suicides inspired by Castell's death, Sakai withdrew from the public eye. She stopped responding to reporters' calls. Her apartment was found vacant, and only her lightest belongings had been removed. On the kitchen floor still glittered the pieces of her shattered camera.

Years later, her younger sister would receive a letter with no return address. The writing was in Mia's airy script, and it said:

> J,
>
> I've missed you. Sorry about the mess. Some must have fallen onto you. I can't ask forgiveness; if I started, I would never stop.
>
> My days pass between glass walls. I've found work at a nursery for exotic plants: wolfsbane, rosary pea, sprigs of oleander, strange violets that mustn't be touched without gloves.
>
> I think I am trying to understand how terrible things grow from small seeds.
>
> When I die, tell no one.
>
> –M.

If she is alive today, Sakai will turn sixty this spring.

At the end of the decade, the number of art-suicides was still measured by the handful, not by the dreadful multitude. It might have remained so, had there been no one to stoke the flames.

The hand that drove the bellows belonged to Otto Bogard (Dec 13, 2002–Oct 9, 2042), a tabloid photographer and mercenary journalist. From his journals, we know the circumstances that ultimately led to his catastrophic involvement.

94

In late 2039, Bogard came into possession of a video recording on which he hoped to make his fortune. The video, taken with a handheld recorder pressed against a steamy windowpane, revealed a scandalous liaison between an Emirati prince and members of his staff. Through a series of threatening letters and ominously placed prints, Bogard attempted to blackmail the prince out of a sum which would have provided for a comfortable retirement.

His offer was not well received, and Bogard soon found himself in blindfolded negotiation with truncheon-wielding men. He was persuaded to accept a lower price, agreeing to destroy all copies of the video in exchange for his life.

After a monthlong hospital stay, Bogard returned to the ransacked site of his apartment, unscrewed his doorbell, and removed the backup card he had stashed there. He sent the video to a publisher in Paris, selling it for a pittance, and made hasty arrangements to depart the continent.

Bogard spent the next two seasick weeks in the steerage of a Grecian freighter, amid the warm animal smells of caged chickens and the constant bleating of goats bemoaning their bellies full of surgically concealed heroin. By day, he subsisted on patsas and ouzo, and by night dreamed strange dreams full of barnyard intrigues.

To avoid discussing the formalities of passports and paperwork with the Port Authority, Bogard leapt overboard half a mile from the coast of Roger's Bay and dog-paddled the rest of the way through storm swells and hissing black rain. He finally climbed the trash-strewn shore and fell gratefully to his knees, bearing nothing but the clothes on his back and a valise full of telephoto lenses. Somewhere, distant thunder rolled.

Bogard had connections in the American paparazzi, and for a time he took assignments snapping pictures of celebrities in sheer dresses or tender poolside moments, but he had grander aspirations, and when he learned of the following that surrounded

Castell's death-portrait, he decided he'd found his inspiration.

For the remaining two years of his life, Bogard dedicated himself to the reporting of art-suicides. He started a chronicle of the phenomenon, coining himself "the Boatman" and signing his reports with the image of a grinning Charon-figure.

He wrote lurid descriptions of the suicides, accompanied whenever possible by photographs and video recordings. His articles were exploitative, sensationalist, and obscenely popular. Within weeks, the Boatman's readership climbed into the millions, and what had been a limited cult of obsession became a national spectacle.

The following examples suffice to demonstrate his approach.[1]

The Amazing Diving Woman

Spectacle in the Sky at 1700 East Avenue! Office drones on their way to the lunch shuffle were surprised to see the Stars and Stripes come fluttering down right on top of their heads. It seems that one Annie Evans decided to redecorate the flagpole on the Drexler building—twenty stories up!

Instead of the classic colors, Annie preferred a gymnastic touch, equipping the outstretched pole with a trapeze swing. She lowered herself onto the bar—and began the performance of a lifetime!

It didn't take long for a crowd to gather below the astounding Ms. Evans, a former aerialist with 15 years' experience. She dazzled the audience with her twists and turnarounds. Gasps rose each time she fell—only to catch the bar with fingertip precision.

Just then, a hooded man—no doubt an incognito colleague of hers—demanded that the captivated onlookers step back "for the installation of crucial safety equipment." He then carefully placed a

---

[1] Out of respect for the deceased, I have falsified the names in the following excerpts, all except one.

teacup full of water on the concrete concourse floor, right below the flagpole.

Annie performed an immaculate dismount and a record-setting octuple somersault, but might have lost a few points on the landing. Both teacup and concourse were greatly impacted, leaving behind quite a crater.

And as for Annie? She'll always be swinging from our heartstrings.

You heard it from the Boatman!

The Scintillated Man

Street artists, you've met your match!

Liam Dorsey was determined to leave his mark in the world–and he found just the alley for it. Using photo-reactive pigment and a roller brush, he spruced up the side of his brownstone building with a fresh coat of paint. Next, the inventive Mr. Dorsey aimed a strobe lamp at the wall, switched it on, and took off running–right through the light's flashing rays.

The result? A series of shadow-cast silhouettes showing a man first jogging, then sprinting, and finally leaping toward the street– right into the path of the 7:38 crosstown bus!

We have to hand it to Mr. Dorsey–he certainly got the exposure he was looking for.

You heard it from the Boatman!

The other articles–over sixty in all–are similarly tasteless.

Through his coverage of the art-suicides, Otto Bogard not only increased their audience a thousandfold, but also fostered a culture of infatuation with death. Tempted by the promise of posthumous fame, aspiring artists emerged in droves, and the number of art-suicides soon soared.

Bogard ignored appeals from the decedents' families, who often asked him to remove content showcasing their loved ones. The Boatman articles faced a series of injunctions and legal embargoes, but Bogard proved resilient in finding new hosts for his features, and his readership followed with him.

There is only one other Boatman article worth noting, and it is the last one ever posted:

The Bottom-Feeder

Life just got a little more interesting for the fish in the Pike River!

On a chilly October night, the infamous Mr. Otto Bogard stopped by his favorite pub–Rowe's Tavern–for a stiff drink. There, he made a lewd comment to the barwoman, as he often did, and ordered a Brandy Sour. He then spent forty-five minutes telling the other patrons about his latest article and the poor overdosed girl it mentioned, during which time he was paying very little attention to his pockets.

Leaving no tip, Mr. Bogard exited the establishment, settled into his car, and began the long downhill drive on Collin Street. How strange it must have seemed, when first he turned his wheel, and found his direction unchanged. As the car picked up speed, Bogard tried to pump life into his brakes, but the pedal only sank to the floor. Rushing forward, now plunging, in a blur of streetlights, he hurtled toward the embankment ahead. Then came the impact, the crack of branches, and–for a moment, weightless flight.

Bogard was always determined to make a splash, and so he did! As the water rose, lapping at the windows, he tried the locks, all of which were jammed. He surely thought to use the safety punch he kept in his glove compartment. What a surprise to find it missing!

By then, the waters of the Pike River had enveloped his car, and the last light of the moon was receding far above. Bogard heard a telltale buzz and saw that his phone had been set with a curious reminder. It seemed that someone had loaded it with a copy of this very article!

He had plenty of time to read it.

Do you think of the people you've put into your pages, Bogard? Can you even remember their names? Are they with you now, swimming through the shadows, staring at you with milk-blind eyes? Was it you who guided them there?

I'd like you to think of my daughter, Boatman. Carry her with you as you cross into the dark. It's the least you can do.

The article was uploaded anonymously on October 10. Authorities declined to investigate Bogard's disappearance as a homicide.

Art-suicide had reached its flashpoint. It spread from shore to shore, finding fuel among the downcast, the outraged, the fame-seekers of every nation. Crucifixions grew so common that pious cities banned the sale of lumber during Lent. Professors in Taipei gave lectures on momentum from atop the tracks of approaching trains, while dancers in Chennai shimmied under scarves of vipers.

Next came the caravans. Over weedy trails and secluded roads they traveled, going by whatever route might hide them from the attentions of the law. These were the first professionals, troupes of performers banded together under such names as The Merry Martyrs or The Taut Rope Repertory Guild. Their goal, so stated, was "to elevate the much-practiced but seldom-studied art of dying."

In a single night they would arrive, play their acts, and vanish before the dawn. They gave performances in public parks, from abandoned theaters, or under the dripping eaves of bridges where derelicts huddled beside drum-barrel fires.

Wherever they chose to perform, their acrobats would throw off their disguises, tumble through the streets, and herald the troupe's arrival with a fanfare of kazoos. In the silence that followed, the crowds mumbled and scratched their heads, and then, when the confusion neared its ripest, the distant strains of calliope music would crawl through the air, and the caravan came trundling along, engines rumbling, electric signs aglow, with painted ladies blowing kisses and launching firework rockets that burst into crackling starlight sparks.

Through the surreal shows that followed, the performers honed their crafts. Each practiced for the day when he would decide to end his career in one last spectacular flourish, when the juggler would trade away his clubs for live grenades, or the escape artist would snap her keys and slip the world outright.

The troupe espoused philosophies that were absurdist and often incoherent, except that they abhorred the idea that death should choose a man, and not the other way around.

They recognized no leader, but there was a first among them: crook-nosed, snaggle-toothed, and ever-grinning beneath his foolscap of violet silk, he was the one they called Chiaro, and they named him patron saint of lunatics and kings.

Chiaro was not a man, but an image, an ideal represented in a ghastly porcelain mask. By turns they took up his name, and wore his face, and gave performances in his honor. These acts were varied and unpredictable, except that they would always end in the actor's own death, at which point the mask would pass to an understudy, who became the next Chiaro, and the cycle would repeat again. By the time it was retired, each mask bore layer upon layer of cuts, gouges, acid-pockmarks, flame scars, and the studs of old shrapnel.

Of all these performances, there were none so infamous as the mortality plays. Little record remains of those macabre scripts, as it was customary to burn all copies after they were staged. Yet one text escaped destruction. It was titled *The Wisdom of the Sot*:

[EXTERIOR - *a park bench beneath the* STATUE OF SOCRATES, *to be played by dear dead Rimbért while his plaster holds.* SAYED *lies prostrate and surrounded by bottles. Enter* ADILLUS, *pushing a squeaky cart.*]

SAYED: O cruel noise! Get that cart away, unless you bring a cure for this damned hangover.

ADILLUS: That, and more besides. But have cheer, good fellow—the night is fine, and every star retains her place. What causes you dismay?

SAYED: It is too cold, I am too sober, and you are here. Come now, you want something–get it out.

ADILLUS: Only to see you smile, my bristly friend.

SAYED: Spare me. Old men have no time for riddles or rogues.

ADILLUS: There's ever a time for either. But lo! If your smile be lost, I have one here!

[ADILLUS *rummages in his cart and produces the* MASK OF CHIARO]

SAYED: What fearful face is this? Hound's teeth, goblin nose, a grin to trick the devil from his final cent–what art would make such a thing?

ADILLUS: I find it charming, myself. Perhaps you prefer the face that greets you at the bottom of a wineglass?

SAYED: You make sport of me.

ADILLUS: Never, sir! Not if all the world were a field, and you the only ball. Pray tell, how fares your father?

SAYED: Dead, God rest his soul.

ADILLUS: Gently so. And your wife, is she with you still?

SAYED: With the plague, she fell.

ADILLUS: Many did. Have you no son?

SAYED: Missing in war, and empty is his grave.

ADILLUS: Wicked fate! It offers alms only so the beggar's the better to rob. Death has followed your every step, has it not?

SAYED: Always.

ADILLUS: Yet you turn away as if it were a stranger. Tell–is he merry, one who looks long upon a banquet, but tastes no morsel; who glimpses sweet wine, but drinks not a drop?

[SAYED slowly takes up the MASK]

SAYED: What are you, truly?

ADILLUS: Three parts dust, a dram of borrowed blood, tomorrow's ashes today. In sum, as much as any man.

[SAYED gazes into the eyes of the MASK]

SAYED: I have sometimes thought I heard, on still nights, a voice calling my name.

ADILLUS: Give it answer.

[SAYED dons the MASK]

SAYED/CHIARO: Light it is to wear, and how easily it fits!

ADILLUS: Indeed you have worn it all your life, though you knew not so.

SAYED/CHIARO: What fine lenses fill these eyes–they show the shape of truth. Why, a crypt's as cozy as a cabin, and the vulture's but a meadowlark in his evening wear. I'll toast, then, to health and other illusions, but where's a drink so worthy?

ADILLUS: How's for a glass of absinthe to tickle a tune from your bones?

SAYED/CHIARO: That won't do–far too green for my sanguine disposition.

[ADILLUS shrugs and flings aside the glass]

ADILLUS: Brandy, then? Not a bad vintage, if Napoleon is to be believed.

SAYED/CHIARO: I've had my fill of candied wine. Have you nothing stronger?

[ADILLUS tosses the bottle away with a crash]

ADILLUS: There's one bitter brew better, if you think it so–a drink to soothe the hearts of jilted lovers and make whole the kingdoms of dethroned kings; one steeped in flowers from the philosopher's grave. Would you slake your thirst on a tea of hemlock?

SAYED/CHIARO: Yes, at last! This is a noble spirit. Here, here– *(to ADILLUS)* Play on, brave piper, play on! *(to the STATUE OF SOCRATES)* Peace, good scholar. Mind not this lended cup–it passes to you soon. *(to audience)* I go before you all, but only by a step. To life!

[SAYED *drinks deep. A cheer from the troupe. Expire* SAYED]

The play was performed, once.

In deep woods, where a quiet clearing lay, the troupe built a pyre. They set the actor's body atop the framework cradle and left lilies in his hair. There they gathered round to watch the fire climb, and sang in the low rolling drone of Lakota prayers, broken by shrill cries and the tinkling of tambourines.

Clouds had shrouded the stars, and no light pierced the dark save for the red blaze rising from the dead man's body. Some passed wine bottles back and forth, or drew from reed-stem pipes that smelled of spice and summer leaves.

They had brought the pages of the script, and these they folded into paper gliders, and threw them so they flew within the fire and emerged on soaring updrafts, trailing plumes of flame that vanished in the night.

Meanwhile, the playwright stood apart. He did not burn his pages, but kept them crumpled in the pocket of his coat. He stared long into the heart of the fire, until the embers grew cold and dawn paled the sky. Then he picked his way across the sleeping and twining forms of the troupe, and left.

It isn't enough. A few preserved pages, the lines of this minor chronicle–sins should be better attested than this.

I owe them more than words alone.

Droplets tap against my windowpane, tracing bright rivulets as they fall. The street below is busy with the milling of the midday crowd, their shadows faint beneath the low and leaden sky. It will rain hard this night, but not before I carry out my act.

I haven't forgotten the face that waits for me, not for a moment since I stole the thing away. Even in dreams, I see the wicked grin, the sickle nose, the hollow spaces for my eyes to fill.

It has waited long enough. Time, now, for the mask to embrace its new wearer.

There.

That's better.

I know what comes next. I have seen this day a thousand times in planning.

First, I gather up the means: my violin, its case, and the revolver concealed within. I have prepared my instruments carefully. The strings are keenly tuned; the gun is clean and ready. There is no chance of misfire. Each element of this act will play its part.

With case in hand, I descend the stairs, cross the street, walk into the crowd. The mask draws stares from those around me. They know what it portends. I find a fitting corner, somewhere well exposed where the sound will carry far. Setting down my case, I open the latches with a steely click. I take up my violin and bow, pausing to savor the rosy smell of the wood, and begin to play a composition that I have practiced every day for the last three years.

The strings hum and sigh and echo through the streets, reaching curious ears, drawing in my audience. Slow and strange, the melody unwinds, laying chord upon chord, note after tender note.

In the last passage of this piece, the central motif repeats in an excruciating diminuendo. My listeners anticipate the final chord, feel it building in their bones. And just before I reach that last note of sweet resolution, I drop my bow, draw the gun, and press the barrel to my temple.

But I do not fire.

The onlookers are confused. Many are disappointed as they

watch me lower the gun, put away the violin, and leave without a spoken word. Some jeer and spit curses after me, demanding I deliver that instant of annihilation they have waited for. But others find meaning in this act. They realize it is a protest, one made through the sparing of a life–an art-survival.

Alone, it isn't much. But we are never really so alone as we seem. We are followed, always, by ripples in our wake. They carry outward, farther than we know, to meet someday with others like themselves, and sway together against the tide.

Too many have traded away their lives, seeking shelter within silence. They have been deceived. That welcoming abyss they so readily embrace is a broken mind's mirage. At the bottom isn't freedom, or glory, or even peace. At the bottom is nothing at all. And the hand that kills takes more than just the life it ends–it burns unwritten books, strips the canvas of its future paint, robs the ear of music yet unheard.

I have no right to preach; I know how sweet that siren song can be. Days come when the bottom doesn't seem so far away, when the sun withholds its heat and all that life can offer is a time to shiver in the naked light.

But days pass.

Though I am filled with flaws, and my steps have often gone astray, this life endures. So I'll mend what I can and try to make something from the pieces left behind. The mask should return, I think, to the ones who made it. I will take it there. And when I do, I will tell them this: That a corpus is not judged by its last work, but by its best, that there is more wonder in even the smallest moments of existence than an eternity of silence, and that it is a better and braver thing to spit in the eye of death, and make beauty out of life.

for K.W.

Sarah L. Byrne is a writer and scientific editor in London, UK. Her short speculative fiction has appeared in various publications including IDEOMANCER and DAILY SCIENCE FICTION. Sarah can be found online at http://sarahbyrne.org

Megan Chaudhuri is a toxicologist by training, a science writer by profession, and a fiction writer by inclination. She lives near Seattle with one husband and two cats. Her fiction has appeared in ANALOG, CROSSED GENRES, and FUTURISTICA, and is forthcoming in other equally awesome places.

Elian Crane's fiction can also be found in COSMIC ROOTS AND ELDRITCH SHORES. He lives in the Pacific Northwest, where he writes from a place between sky and sea.

Diana Estigarribia is a science fiction and fantasy writer who traverses the wormhole known as New York City. Her fiction has appeared in HELIOS QUARTERLY MAGAZINE, THE MAIN STREET RAG and other anthologies. Diana received her BFA in Dramatic Writing from Tisch School of the Arts, and in 2009 her play, *"Help Wanted,"* was a finalist for the BBC International Radio Playwriting Competition. She's a VONA VOICES WORKSHOP alumna. Currently she's crafting a trilogy of novels, web serial, and a dozen stories, and wonders if cloning technology is a viable option. Find her online at http://dianaewrites.com and on Twitter @Dhyana_Writes.

Shariann Lewitt is the author of seventeen novels and about forty short stories. She is a graduate of the Yale School of Drama.

Richard C. Rogers lives in Brooklyn with his wife and one cat. His blog about the writing life can be found at
http://rcrogers33.wordpress.com

Matthew Sanborn Smith is a New England expatriate living in Florida whose fiction has appeared at TOR.COM, NATURE, DIABOLICAL PLOTS, and CHIZINE, among others. He is the keeper of the BEWARE THE HAIRY MANGO podcast.

Nick Tchan (writing as Nick T. Chan) is a writer from Sydney, Australia. He's sold stories to ORSON SCOTT CARD'S INTERGALACTIC MEDICINE SHOW, WRITERS OF THE FUTURE, LIGHTSPEED, and GALAXY'S EDGE. In addition to random and malicious acts of authoring, Nick works as an instructional designer for a community investment consultancy. He and his wife also attempt to raise a small child who has already surpassed at least him in intelligence. Because he does not own a cat, he has long doubted his legitimacy as a speculative fiction writer.

Coming Soon!

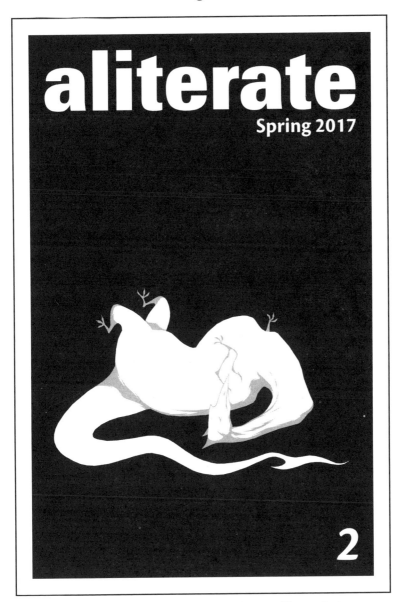

Typeset with X_ƎL^AT_EX in **Minion Pro**, **Cronos Pro**, and **Univers**.